A VICTIM OF CIRCUMSTANCE

A TANNER NOVEL - BOOK 22

REMINGTON KANE

INTRODUCTION

A VICTIM OF CIRCUMSTANCE – A TANNER NOVEL – BOOK 22

What should have been a simple hit turns into a struggle to survive and a race against the clock for Tanner.

ACKNOWLEDGMENTS

I write for you.

—Remington Kane

1
LIKE CLOCKWORK

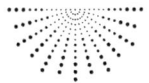

TANNER, SEATED AT THE COUNTER INSIDE A DINER IN Byzantine, West Virginia, watched as one of the waitresses slipped into the men's room.

It was Friday morning and he had been staying in the town of eighteen thousand for two days in preparation of making a hit. Byzantine, West Virginia was without doubt the most unscrupulous and corrupt town he had ever been to. And Tanner had once lived in Las Vegas.

Upon his arrival, he had gone less than a mile into the town when a police officer pulled him over. The cop, who was in his twenties and overweight, wore a soiled uniform shirt along with jeans and sneakers.

Tanner assumed he had wandered into some unmarked small-town speed trap. He had. The cop claimed that a section of the road had a limit of only fifteen miles an hour. When Tanner asked the man where the speed limit was posted, the cop pointed to a road sign nailed to a tree. The sign was no bigger than a memo card and too small to be read without binoculars.

Tanner took the ticket without complaint. It was bad

enough he had been seen by a cop, he didn't need to become memorable. He was breaking one of his own rules by hanging around the town where he was to make a hit. Worse yet, he'd taken a room there. It couldn't be avoided.

The other hotels and motels in the area were full. There were a pair of conventions taking place in the area and one of the larger hotels had recently suffered a fire and was temporarily closed. If he had more time to plan, Tanner would have booked accommodations outside the town of Byzantine.

The contract came to him with a fat fee and a time limit attached. He was given four days to kill his target, a man named Jack Bellamy.

Bellamy had committed financial fraud while he was the head of a top hedge fund. Yet, Bellamy hadn't served a day in jail. Instead, he'd placed the blame on his compliance officer and the fund's chief financial officer.

Jack Bellamy was tainted and disgraced by the scandal. Although he shouted his innocence in interviews, those in the know were aware that he alone was to blame. His compliance officer and his C.F.O. had been made dupes by the man.

Once it became obvious that his legal shenanigans had been uncovered, Bellamy went to the Securities and Exchange Commission and made a deal. He would incriminate his colleagues to save himself. His personal fortune was several hundred million and the only financial penalty he faced was a relatively small fine.

The hedge fund failed. The wealthiest shareholders managed to get their money returned. However, thousands of smaller investors lost everything, and it was because of Bellamy's actions.

That the man was unrepentant became obvious when he gave an interview in which he called his victims,

"Amateurs who should have stayed out of the market and let the big boys play."

Tanner routinely took contracts on those who had harmed others through violent means rather than financial. Still, a scumbag was a scumbag, and Tanner agreed to put Bellamy down.

Tanner was in town under the guise of being a real estate developer named Paul Diehl. Byzantine had dilapidated lakeside cabins that were sitting vacant. The owner was looking to sell to someone who would revitalize or rebuild the property. It was a good cover identity and gave Tanner a reason to be in town.

THE WAITRESS EXITED THE MEN'S ROOM WHILE PLACING A stick of chewing gum in her mouth. Seconds later, a man in a work uniform came out too. The man was wearing a satisfied smile on his face. Tanner had been propositioned by the same cute waitress. She had asked him if he liked what he saw and offered to butter more than his toast.

Tanner declined, and he had observed that his waitress and one other server hooked on the side. When he watched the women pass along money to the man who owned the diner, Tanner realized the part-time prostitution was encouraged.

At the Byzantine Hotel, where he was staying, the bell boys sold drugs while the maids committed petty theft. Tanner had placed a hidden camera in his room and caught one of the maids going through his things. The woman had taken a pair of cheap sunglasses and had the audacity to wear them in front of him. Tanner didn't report the theft. He just wanted to fulfill his contract and leave the corrupt town behind him.

To that end, Tanner had spent two days getting to know his target and his habits. He had been helped by the client, who had revealed the location of Jack Bellamy's love nest. Bellamy, who was forty-four, was married to a beautiful twenty-three-year-old redhead named Melissa. Melissa was Bellamy's fourth wife. Despite his wife's obvious attributes, Bellamy had an equally stunning mistress named Tiffany Hayes. Tiffany was also in her twenties, blonde, and gorgeous.

The love nest was a bungalow-style house in a secluded location. It had three bedrooms, two baths, and a finished basement. There was a well-stocked bar, a jacuzzi, and a huge wall-mounted TV. A large picture window at the front of the home looked out onto the wraparound porch. Tanner decided it would be a good location to make the kill.

Tiffany had left the love nest first the previous day, leaving Bellamy behind and alone. Tanner had been tempted to kill the man at that time, but he had yet to follow through on the procedures he used whenever making a hit. He had to scout the area surrounding the home and evaluate the probability of anyone being near enough to see anything. Once he fired the shot that would kill Bellamy, the noise would travel, sound suppressor or not. It likely wouldn't be a problem, since no one would be near enough to pinpoint where the shot came from.

Tanner also had to make plans for escape in the event he walked into a trap or something went wrong. He had learned years earlier through painful experience that it was important to prepare for every contingency.

There was also the reason for his visit to the area to consider. To keep his cover up, Tanner had met with the man selling the lakefront property. The man had extolled the virtues of the lake and its great fishing until Tanner told him he knew the lake was devoid of fish because it had become contaminated.

"How did you find out about that?" the man asked. He was an older gentleman with a grandfatherly face.

"I did some research before coming to town. The lake would have to be drained and cleaned before anyone could live here. I'm also aware that the cabins have termite damage. Given that, your asking price is much too high."

The man had sent him a wink. "I'll find the right sucker to buy it, you watch."

Tanner wondered then if everyone in the town was corrupt in some way. Jack Bellamy might be the community's most notorious native scoundrel, but he was certainly not it's only one.

TANNER LEFT THE DINER AND DROVE TO THE AREA WHERE Bellamy would soon be meeting with his lover. The client had given him four days to kill Bellamy and half of that had already gone by. Tanner spent the next three hours preparing for the hit, with the final hour used to scout the surrounding area. There was no one else around. The nearest home was on the other side of the road and half a mile away.

Tanner settled in atop the small hill he had picked out for a firing position. He was pleased to see the car that belonged to Bellamy's mistress sitting beside Jack Bellamy's white Jaguar.

Tanner had expected a longer wait, but the young woman appeared in the doorway twenty-six minutes later, with Bellamy at her side. They shared a passionate kiss before she got into her car and drove away.

Tanner had sighted in on Tiffany as she walked toward

her vehicle and admired her through his scope. The blonde was an exceptional beauty. Bellamy had good taste, if not good sense.

After Tiffany left, Tanner watched Bellamy move around by spying on him through the picture window. The man was wearing a white dress shirt with no tie and his slacks were black. Bellamy had made himself a drink and was sipping on it. Jack Bellamy had dark hair, brown eyes, was bearded, and stood five-foot-ten. His build was average, and he stayed trim despite never exercising.

Tanner was about to pull the trigger on Bellamy when the man moved away from the window. It was of little consequence. Bellamy had opened the front door and stepped outside. He walked several yards away from the home, then stopped and took a sip of his drink. Bellamy was gazing around at the fine spring day when Tanner placed four rounds in his chest. The high-velocity slugs tore apart Bellamy's lungs, heart, and severed his spine.

The man who had abused his power and lost millions for the people who trusted him fell backwards and settled on the driveway. The law might have dealt leniently with him, but Tanner's employer wasn't as forgiving, and Bellamy had paid for his transgressions.

Tanner smiled as he left the area. The contract was fulfilled, and he could leave the shady little town of Byzantine behind him.

Unfortunately for Tanner, he was wrong on both counts.

2
SEE YOURSELF AS OTHERS DO

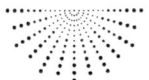

ONE HOUR EARLIER

WHILE TANNER HAD BEEN SCOUTING THE AREA IN preparation for making the hit, Jack Bellamy had arrived at the secluded home to meet his mistress. Tiffany's green Mazda was already there, and Bellamy parked beside it.

This would be only his third meeting with Tiffany, whom he had met while he was out cruising bars in a nearby town. The woman caught the eye of every man in the room when she'd entered the sports bar, but Bellamy had been the first to buy her a drink. An hour later they were in a motel room.

Bellamy had no delusions about himself. He wasn't ugly, but neither was he a male model. Tiffany was seeing him because he was rich and could buy her things. She had already gotten an expensive diamond bracelet out of him, and he would buy her more things as long as they were together.

Women themselves were things to Bellamy, as were

most of the people he interacted with. He respected no one, and life was all about having fun and getting richer.

He had been ruthless and conniving since he was a child and was proud of it. Bellamy considered those attributes as being the main qualities that had taken him from poverty to extreme wealth. It never seemed to occur to him that his lack of empathy and love of deceit might be the cause of his downfall.

Sure, he may have been a bit too greedy when he came up with that scheme to defraud that ruined his hedge fund. Still, he'd been wise enough to take out insurance by dragging others along with him. He had talked two of his fund's executives into helping him with the promise of making them more money than they had ever seen before.

As soon as things went south, Bellamy called the authorities and asked to make a deal. Bellamy claimed he was innocent of any wrongdoing, but that he knew the names of the ones responsible. No one believed in his innocence, nonetheless, a deal was struck that enabled him to remain free. As for his partners, they were still serving time and had years to go on their sentences.

Bellamy didn't escape completely unscathed. His reputation was ruined, and his company dismantled. He'd also had to pay a fine of a hundred and eighty thousand dollars. The fine was but a fraction of the money he'd hidden in foreign banks and meant nothing, nor was he concerned about the hit his reputation had taken. What caused Bellamy pain was being told he could never run another financial institution.

His lack of ethics and empathy aside, Bellamy was a true genius when it came to financial matters. He loved high finance and wheeling and dealing. He had found a way around the ban by acting as a secret advisor to an old friend he'd grown up with in Byzantine, a man named Grant Dixon.

His recommendations had increased Dixon's modest portfolio by a hundred-fold. Later on, Bellamy's gift at investing gave Dixon the reputation on Wall Street of being a top market analyst. Dixon was also considered a genius by many. Those accolades rightly belonged to Bellamy. And he had a plan to see that he was acknowledged.

To confess that he was the true wizard behind the curtain was a risky act that could see Bellamy serve time. Without doubt it would ruin Dixon and turn him into a joke. Jack Bellamy didn't give a damn what happened to Dixon, his oldest friend. What he couldn't abide was being thought of as a has-been, not when he had built one of the most successful hedge funds of all time and knew that he could do so again. His ego was about to override his good sense. In some ways, it was the story of Jack Bellamy's life.

BELLAMY ENTERED HIS LOVE NEST AND HALTED INSIDE THE doorway. Sounds were coming from the bedroom. They were noises he had expected to hear, but only as a participant. It was the sound of lovemaking. Bellamy eased the front door shut and crept toward the bedroom. The home was furnished with sofas and chairs in a traditional style and had a fireplace that ran on propane.

The thick braided rug on the floor helped to muffle his footsteps. As he moved closer to the bedroom doorway, Bellamy found himself aroused by the obvious sounds of pleasure coming from Tiffany.

Tiffany was smart enough not to ruin a good thing. She wouldn't be screwing some other guy in his bed, especially when he was expected at any moment. That meant that she might have talked a woman into joining them in their fun. If so, Bellamy approved.

Jack Bellamy eased one eye around the door frame of the bedroom. What he saw made him gasp. There *was* a man in bed with Tiffany. They were both naked and making love. Yes, it was a man, but not just any man.

Bellamy gave up trying to be stealthy and entered the room with his mouth hanging open in shock. He told himself that what he was seeing wasn't possible, and yet, he kept on seeing it. Tiffany had her back to him as she rode the man beneath her.

The guy smiled up at Bellamy as he approached the bed. The man could have been Bellamy's twin.

"How? What?" Bellamy said. Then a bright white light erupted inside his skull, and Jack Bellamy fell to the floor.

TIFFANY CLIMBED OFF HER LOVER AFTER HITTING BELLAMY with a powerful stun gun. Before the man could recover, she removed a syringe from the bedside table and used it on Bellamy. The ex-titan of Wall Street began snoring as drool leaked from the corner of his mouth.

Bellamy's double, a man named Carl Leffler, climbed out of bed and put on a robe.

"We got him, baby. And did you get a look at his face? He thought he was seeing things. If I can trick him, everyone else will be fooled too."

Leffler was nine years younger than Bellamy and their resemblance was only superficial. Nonetheless, Leffler was a master at changing his appearance.

Tiffany fastened her own robe as she stared down at Bellamy. "I wish we really could ransom him for a million dollars. It's a shame we'll only be faking his kidnapping."

"That million won't matter, not after two days go by. All we have to do is keep him on ice and we'll all make millions."

Tiffany grabbed a computer tablet and composed a quick email. "I'll tell the others to come and get him."

Within minutes, two men showed up. They were Rudy and Larry. Rudy was thirty-six, had blond hair and brown eyes, while Larry was twenty-nine and had brown hair and blue eyes. Both men were around six-feet tall. They stared at Carl Leffler, then down at Bellamy.

"Damn, but you two look alike," Rudy said. "Are you sure you drugged the right man, Tiffany?"

They carried an unconscious Jack Bellamy outside and deposited him into the rear of a small truck.

AFTER RUDY AND LARRY LEFT, TIFFANY AND CARL GOT dressed as they went over the plan again.

"You're sure you can pull it off? You look like Jack Bellamy, but you don't sound like him," Tiffany said.

Carl kissed her. "Relax, baby, you know I won't push my luck. I'll just go to that bar he likes to hang out at and make sure I'm seen by several witnesses."

"But someone will try to talk to you."

Carl let his face go slack and spoke as if he were drunk. "I'll just pretend to be plastered and slur my words. It will make me more memorable."

"Okay, and afterwards?"

"I abandon Bellamy's ride nearby and head to that place we picked out."

"And what comes before that?"

Carl looked confused for a moment, but then he smiled. "I leave the ransom note inside the car, so the cops will think he was grabbed after leaving the bar."

"Yes, and that will give all of us time to set up our alibis."

"Even if we're suspected they won't be able to prove a thing."

Tiffany kissed Carl, then patted his bearded cheek. "I'll be glad when you take off this disguise. I'm sick of kissing Jack Bellamy."

"You did more than kiss him."

"Don't be jealous; it was all a part of the plan."

"That doesn't mean I have to like it."

Tiffany smiled. "I'll make it up to you."

Carl stared at her, into her eyes, and frowned at what he was seeing.

"Why are you looking at me like that?" Tiffany asked.

"You're back on the blow. I can tell by the way your eyes look."

"I just snorted a little to get through the day. This kidnapping plot is more dangerous than the usual cons we run. If we get caught we'll all be in a federal prison."

"You promised me, Tiffany. You said you were off the cocaine for good."

"I know, and I will be once this is over, and we get paid."

Carl gave her a doubtful look, but he didn't say anything else on the subject.

When she was ready to go, Leffler walked Tiffany to the door and kissed her goodbye. He didn't have to leave for the bar for another few hours and had time to kill.

After mixing himself a drink, he took a stroll outside and looked around.

Carl Leffler, a former actor turned con artist, was indeed a master of disguise. So much so that he fooled the assassin who was out to kill the man he was pretending to be. Leffler died in Jack Bellamy's place, leaving Tanner none the wiser.

3

A CHANGE OF PLANS

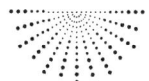

IN THE HOURS AFTER THE HIT, TIFFANY HAD CALLED CARL several times and received no answer, not even a text. Fearing something may have gone wrong, she returned to the bungalow. That was when she discovered Carl's body. After weeping over her lover, she called Rudy and Larry. When they arrived on the scene, their faces revealed the shock Tiffany was feeling.

"What the fuck?" Rudy said. "Who would kill Carl?"

Larry shook his head as he pointed down at the body. "That's Carl, but he doesn't look like himself. I think somebody thought they were killing Jack Bellamy."

"What?" Tiffany said, as she wiped at her eyes.

"Yeah," Rudy said. "That makes sense, and lots of people hate Bellamy."

"Shit. What does this do to the plan?" Larry said. "Now none of us have an alibi for when Bellamy goes missing."

"We have to call Melissa," Tiffany said, "or better yet, let's tell her to come here. This was all her idea in the first place."

"You think she'll come?" Rudy asked.

"She'll come," Tiffany said, "and knowing her she'll think of something."

A HALF HOUR LATER, MELISSA BELLAMY ARRIVED AND looked down at the dead form of a man who resembled her husband. The kidnapping had been Melissa's idea, and she had called upon her friends to help her pull it off. The fact was, there really was no kidnapping, or rather, although Bellamy had been abducted, the group holding him had no intention of collecting a ransom. Most kidnappers are caught when it comes time to get their hands on the money. Once the authorities know where to leave the ransom, they also know where the kidnappers will appear to collect it.

The whole idea of Bellamy's abduction was to put him out of commission for a few days. Melissa had signed a prenuptial agreement which stated she would get nothing if Jack divorced her or died within their first three years of marriage.

Cruel bastard that he is, Bellamy was waiting until the last moment to start proceedings. He had done the same thing to wives' number two and number three, and Melissa had found out about it. However, if the marriage lasted beyond the three-year mark, the contract stated that Melissa would receive three million dollars. The plan was to keep Bellamy captive until the deadline passed. It was a date that was only two days away.

Knowing she would come under suspicion once it became known how fortuitous the timing of the kidnapping was for her, Melissa came up with a plan. That plan involved Carl Leffler masquerading as her husband to obscure the true time of Bellamy's abduction. With Leffler dead, Melissa's friends had no alibi.

"We can fix this," Melissa said. She was a redhead, petite, and had a shapely body that had lured many a victim of her con games to a sad fate.

Tiffany flushed crimson with anger. "You can't fix anything! Carl is dead."

Melissa reached out and touched her friend's cheek. "Oh, honey, I'm so sorry for your loss, and you know I loved Carl too. That said, we have to move forward with the plan or we'll all be screwed."

"How do we do that?" Rudy asked.

Melissa sighed as she stared down at the body. "I have an idea."

THAT NIGHT, MELISSA BELLAMY DROVE HER HUSBAND'S Jaguar into the parking lot of a restaurant in a neighboring town. Rudy pulled up alongside her in a small truck, which was a converted van. The truck was there to block the view of anyone leaving the restaurant. It would be moved once Melissa and Rudy set the scene.

Carl Leffler's body was buckled in beside Melissa. Despite having driven with the windows down, the corpse gave off an odor that caused Melissa to stop and vomit twice along the trip.

On Leffler's hands were clear latex gloves, just in case the body was still capable of leaving behind fingerprints. Beneath the jacket the corpse wore, the torso had been wrapped in plastic so that no blood would be left behind in the car.

Rudy helped Melissa unbuckle the body and move it over to the driver's seat. Instead of placing it behind the wheel of the vehicle, they made it look as if it were hanging half in and half out of the car. The plan was to give the appearance that Bellamy had driven to the restaurant while drunk. That was an activity that would not be out of character for Jack Bellamy.

Once the body was staged, Rudy wished Melissa luck and drove off in the truck. Melissa then put on a show as she berated her "husband's" behavior.

"Damn it, Jack! You nearly hit that light pole on the way in here. You're too drunk to be out in public, much less drive a car."

A pair of older couples who were leaving the restaurant together took notice of the scene, although they were too far away to make out details. Another couple who had just arrived at the restaurant walked over to offer Melissa a hand with her husband. It was Tiffany and Larry, who were there to play their parts.

Larry pretended to be helping the body to stand, while straining to hold it upright. He guided the corpse back to the other side of the car, as Melissa and Tiffany obscured the view of the onlookers. After settling the body back in the passenger seat and strapping it in again, Larry laughed aloud as if Bellamy had said something funny.

"Ha, that's a good one, Mr. Bellamy."

Melissa thanked Tiffany and Larry for their help and hollered at her husband again.

"I should make you sleep in the car when we get home!"

After getting behind the wheel, Melissa drove off, as Tiffany and Larry entered the restaurant to establish their alibis. The restaurant was on the ground floor of a hotel. Once they'd eaten their meal, Tiffany and Larry would get a room in the hotel and stay the night.

Rudy, who had parked nearby on a dirt road, was

waiting for Melissa when she arrived. The two of them hustled Carl Leffler's body into the rear of the small delivery truck.

"What will you do with the body?" Melissa asked.

"I know just the place to hide it until it's safe to move him again."

"All right, but don't take too long. Remember, you'll need an alibi too."

"I'll have one. I'm headed to that new casino that just opened up an hour from here. I plan to get a room there and do a little gambling. Maybe I'll even get lucky and win some dough."

"Good luck," Melissa said.

"You too," Rudy said.

THE REAL JACK BELLAMY HAD WOKEN FROM HIS DRUG-induced stupor to find himself locked inside a small space. It was a closet, or it had been before someone reinforced the walls with sheets of plywood. Bellamy had been lying on the floor when he'd awakened.

Beside him was a bucket, a case of spring water, and a box of protein bars. His last memories were confusing, as he recalled watching himself in bed with Tiffany. He concluded that it had been a dream, or a hallucination caused by whatever drug he'd been knocked-out with. After coming fully awake, Bellamy pounded on the steel door of his makeshift cell.

"Hey! What the hell is going on? Is anyone out there?"

There was silence, but just as Bellamy was thinking he was alone, a voice spoke from the other side of the door.

"You have been kidnapped. If you don't cause any trouble, you'll be back home soon."

The tone of speech was mechanical, as if the person speaking were using some sort of device to alter their real voice. That made Bellamy wonder if he knew the person. There was a thin gap beneath the door. Light was visible, except at two spots, where the feet of the person on the other side caused shadows. Bellamy placed his face close to the floor, hoping to get a look at his captor. The gap was too small to make out more than the bottoms of a pair of red sneakers.

"How much money are you asking for me?"

"One million dollars," the voice said.

"Hell, my lawyer should be able to raise that in no time, but I'll tell you what, let me go and I'll give you two million. What do you say?"

"Just do as you're told, and you'll be released soon."

Bellamy got up from the floor, realized he had to pee, and put the bucket to good use. When he was done, he tipped it toward the door to send the urine spilling out beneath the crack.

From the other side of the door came the shuffle of feet and a curse spoken in that strange mechanical voice.

"Lick that up, will you?" Bellamy said, followed by a laugh. On the other side of the door, Bellamy's half-brother, a nineteen-year-old kid named Sammy Bellamy was wondering what he'd let Melissa talk him into.

AFTER ARRIVING HOME TO HER ESTATE, MELISSA BELLAMY drove through the iron gates and parked the Jaguar in the circular driveway. Before going inside the Georgian style mansion, she left the passenger door sitting open, and taped the envelope containing the ransom note to the windshield. To add a touch of starkness to the scene she was creating, Melissa placed one of Bellamy's shoes near the car.

She showered and changed into a nightgown. When she returned to her bedroom, she went over everything in her mind once more. She was certain the new plan should work as well as the old one would have.

In the morning, she would awake to find her husband missing and a ransom note left behind. She imagined the questions the cops would ask her.

"Did you hear anything, Mrs. Bellamy?"

No, she did not, but she had taken a sleeping pill before lying down.

"Why did you leave your husband outside in the car?"

Jack was too heavy to move, and she figured he would wander inside after he sobered up a little.

"Weren't you afraid he might drive off?"

She took the car keys, so he couldn't do that. When she awoke, she realized that her husband had never come into the house, then found the ransom note taped to the inside of the windshield.

Why didn't your alarm system wake you when the front gate was opened?

Jack always sets the alarm before coming to bed. She never does it.

In a house this size, don't you employ a cook or a maid?

The woman who cooks and cleans has the day off.

I see cameras outside the home. That should help us identify the kidnappers and establish the exact time the abduction took place.

Jack bought the phony type that just look like real cameras. He said they were good enough.

∼

Melissa smiled. She would answer any questions the authorities threw at her and weather their skepticism and suspicion. Someone might get the idea she became fed up with Jack and disposed of him somewhere, then came up with the kidnapping story. But once the authorities received a photo of Jack alive and held captive, they would forget her and focus on finding the people who took her husband.

In two days' time, Melissa would reach the three-year mark of her marriage and become eligible to receive three million dollars. It had not escaped Melissa's notice that she might receive considerably more if Jack were to be killed by his captors. She wasn't certain what was in his will, but she thought she might at least wind up with their estate in the event of his untimely and tragic death.

Jack Bellamy had taken Melissa for just another trophy wife he could use and discard. Had he known about Melissa's true past as a con artist, he might have realized they were more alike than he thought.

Melissa drifted off to sleep while dreaming of the riches that awaited her.

4
SAY WHAT?

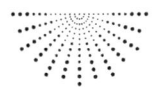

Tanner learned of Jack Bellamy's kidnapping the next morning as he was preparing to check out of his hotel room. He was in the bathroom shaving when he heard Bellamy's name mentioned on a local a.m. news program. Assuming the story would be about the man's death, he walked out of the bathroom and turned the sound up on the television.

To his amazement, the news report was stating that Jack Bellamy had been kidnapped sometime during the previous night. Tanner's first thought was that someone was running a con of some sort after having discovered Bellamy's body.

He began to suspect there was more to the story when a related report came on. That story spoke of Jack Bellamy and his wife being spotted at a restaurant just hours before the kidnapping took place. Someone on the scene had filmed what appeared to be a drunken Bellamy being placed back in his car, after having passed out.

A patron of the restaurant had captured the spectacle by using their phone. And yes, the man being jostled into the car did resemble Bellamy, but Bellamy was dead. Tanner knew there was no way the man could have survived the four rounds he'd put through him.

When he realized the female member of the couple helping Melissa Bellamy was Jack Bellamy's mistress, Tiffany, Tanner was certain a con was in the works. It surprised him that Bellamy's wife was working a game with her husband's mistress, but then, he'd seen stranger partnerships before.

Whatever was going on, it was a problem for Tanner. He had left a message for the client telling him that Bellamy was dead, but now it looked as if he had lied.

If the kidnapping story was allowed to stand, it would appear that Tanner had failed to fulfill a contract. No Tanner had ever failed to deliver on a contract. Lie that it was, Tanner would be damned if he was going to let it be perceived as the truth. The deadline for the Bellamy contract was up at noon the next day. Tanner had until then to expose the kidnapping as a fraud and prove that Bellamy was already dead. He finished shaving, got dressed, and headed out to find Tiffany.

MARTIN GREENE, THE CHIEF OF POLICE OF BYZANTINE, was informed of the kidnapping within minutes of the call coming in. Learning that Jack Bellamy had been abducted put the fear of God in the chief. Chief Greene was fifty-four and a lifelong bachelor. He had sandy hair, blue eyes, acne scars, a deep voice, and stood six-foot-two. Since becoming chief, Greene never wore a uniform, he preferred suits.

Greene's fear came from the fact that he was being blackmailed by Jack Bellamy and had been for several years. Bellamy had information on Greene that the chief found so embarrassing that he would rather die than have it revealed. Bellamy didn't extort money from the man, rather, he insisted that he and those closest to him be allowed to go unmolested by the town's police force.

That arrangement had come in handy for Bellamy a year earlier when he'd run down an elderly man during a hit and run incident. The old man lived but needed a new hip. Chief Greene covered for Bellamy and arranged to have the damage to his car repaired without insurance paperwork being filed.

There were also multiple passes at DUI stops, and once, the chief roughed up a young man who'd had the audacity to insult Bellamy in public. Bellamy was responsible for the man's parents going bankrupt after they had invested heavily in his hedge fund.

The chief, while wearing a mask, had broken the young man's kneecaps and told him to never say a bad word about Jack Bellamy again. Chief Greene despised Bellamy and would snuff the man's life out in an instant if he could get away with it. However, Bellamy had taken out insurance. If anything, *anything*, were to happen to him, what he had on the chief would be made public within a week.

Bellamy had warned the chief that he had arranged it so everyone would learn the chief's secret via a mass emailing. If that happened, Chief Greene knew his life would be over, and that he might also die of embarrassment.

Hoping to get Bellamy back safely as soon as possible, Chief Greene had requested the FBI be brought in on the kidnapping investigation. When two special agents showed up with a small army of personnel just after nine a.m., Chief Greene felt optimistic that Bellamy would be found.

~

Melissa greeted the two lead FBI agents and wondered if they were twins. When she realized through their conversation that one of them was a woman, she still wasn't sure which of the pair that was. The special agents both had short brown hair, brown eyes, and were dressed in bland gray suits with white shirts and black ties.

Their names offered little hope in Melissa distinguishing one from the other. They were similar, and Melissa couldn't keep them straight in her mind. They were FBI Special Agent Dana Williams–Male, and FBI Special Agent Jamie Willis – Female.

The androgynous Feds appeared competent and went by the book. They both assured Melissa, in their eerily identical voices that they were determined to get Bellamy back and catch the kidnappers. Melissa thanked them while hoping they wouldn't be trouble for her.

~

NASHVILLE, TENNESSEE

The man who'd hired Tanner to kill Jack Bellamy was Grant Dixon. Dixon was forty-four, with dark hair and a swimmer's physique. He had known Bellamy since the two of them were in diapers. Like Bellamy, Dixon had majored in finance and went off after college to make his fortune in New York City.

Unlike Bellamy, Grant Dixon was no financial wizard. While Bellamy was making multi-million-dollar trades on Wall Street, Dixon worked for a financial services company as a loan officer. Dixon had later attended law school as he sought to change careers.

Bellamy made his first ten million dollars before the age of twenty-seven. At that same time, Dixon, sick of big city life, had moved back home to Byzantine to open a law firm.

Dixon was successful at his new career and was making a good living. In time, he'd gained a reputation as being a fine defense lawyer. When Bellamy moved back to Byzantine after narrowly escaping going to prison, the two men reconnected.

Bellamy later talked Dixon into acting as a front man for him in the financial arena. That decision was advantageous beyond Dixon's dreams and made him a millionaire a hundred times over. He soon became recognized as a financial guru and was the go-to guy for market analysis by news outlets. Dixon was also on the verge of signing a lucrative book deal.

Although Bellamy was the true genius behind Dixon's success, Dixon always figured he was helping out Bellamy as much as Bellamy was helping him. It was because of him that Jack Bellamy was still able to wheel and deal, even if he had to do so through a surrogate.

Any other man would have counted himself lucky and stayed quiet, but oh no, not Jack Bellamy. Dixon had learned through a source in television news that Bellamy had arranged to give an interview to a print reporter from the country's leading financial magazine. The interview was to take place in New York City in five days, and Bellamy had made reservations to travel there.

Grant Dixon knew his old friend well. As smart as Bellamy was when it came to finance, his ego always found a way to get him into trouble. The fool had set up the interview to reveal that he was the brains behind Dixon's rise to success. Not only might that land Bellamy in more hot water, but Dixon would look like a stooge. Dixon wasn't going to let that happen, so he arranged to hire Tanner, then went on a last-minute vacation to Nashville with his girlfriend.

It was said that once you employed Tanner you could consider the target dead. That had seemed true the day before when he received word through an email drop that Bellamy had been killed. And yet, upon awakening, Dixon had seen the story of Bellamy's kidnapping.

A part of Dixon had rejoiced at hearing Jack was still alive. They had been friends forever and he liked the man a great deal. He was the only person who could say that, and still he wanted Bellamy dead.

After finding himself too nervous to stay in Nashville, Dixon made up a story for his girlfriend about a law client needing him. He was heading back home to Byzantine to get the local scuttlebutt on the kidnapping.

Despite any feelings of remorse or guilt Dixon might feel over having Bellamy killed, he still needed him gone. Whether he was slain by Tanner or killed by the people who kidnapped him, Dixon's greatest hope was that Jack Bellamy would soon be dead.

5
MOUSE TRAP

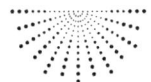

IN THE DAYS LEADING UP TO THE HIT, TANNER HAD LEARNED where Bellamy's mistress, Tiffany Hayes lived. She was renting an apartment on the second floor of a three-story building that looked as if it were a converted warehouse. It was located along the town's main drag.

Tanner was in his rental vehicle down the block from where Tiffany's green Mazda was parked. He was watching a small drama play out on the opposite side of the street and several doors away.

A little blonde girl with the face of an angel was attempting to coax her kitten out of a tree. She had asked several people to help her with the orange tabby, but they had all walked past her without so much as a smile. The innocent child was the only normal citizen Tanner had come across in Byzantine. If there wasn't the chance that he might miss Tiffany by doing so, Tanner would have left his car and helped the girl free her kitten from the tree. He was still considering the idea when Tiffany came into view and headed toward her vehicle. Tanner placed his car in gear and followed after her.

He was operating under the belief that Jack Bellamy was dead. Melissa Bellamy, along with her husband's mistress, and others, was keeping that fact hidden so that they could stage a phony kidnapping.

Tanner wouldn't have cared about any of it if his credibility wasn't on the line. If it were to be believed that he had failed to fulfill a contract, the reputation he'd built up would cease to exist. He hoped to follow Tiffany to the others involved in the scheme and find out where they had hidden or buried Bellamy's body.

He held no hard feelings against them and would let them live unless they were foolish. It was Tanner's experience that con artists, grifters, and the just plain sneaky were predominately opposed to committing violence. They would rather lie, cheat, and steal to get their way.

As Tiffany drove along on the road out of town she was speaking to someone on a cell phone. Tanner wondered who it was.

Tiffany was talking to Larry, and they were planning a trap for Tanner. They had no idea who had killed Carl while thinking he was Bellamy. They did know there was a good chance that whomever had committed the act also knew about Tiffany, since she had been at the bungalow.

If they were in the assassin's shoes, they would want answers after learning that Bellamy was reportedly still alive and the victim of a kidnapping. That same person would also be a loose end that could ruin their plans.

Both Larry and Tiffany had killed before, although they had done so in self-defense. A mark they had once scammed out of a considerable amount of money had spotted Larry inside a mall and followed him home. The man kept an eye on the rented house for several days with the help of two friends, then made his move when Tiffany arrived at the home.

At the time, Larry had been working a scam with Tiffany and Melissa. When the men broke in with guns extended, Larry had hidden inside the empty cabinets beneath the countertop in the kitchen. In a normal house, there would have been pots, pans, and various clutter taking up the space where Larry hid. However, the rented house was being used as a stage by the con artists for their latest mark. Other than a few used appliances and furniture bought from a thrift shop, the home was vacant of belongings.

Their attackers were so accustomed to thinking of kitchen cabinets as being full that they never looked inside them. After Melissa and Tiffany claimed that Larry had left out the back door and was in the detached garage, one of the men left to look for him.

With surprise on his side, Larry attacked the remaining two men from behind and knocked them to the floor. After a mad scramble to get the guns the men had dropped, Larry shot their former mark while Tiffany fired on one of his friends. When the other friend burst through the rear door wondering what had happened, Tiffany sent three bullets into his chest. Instead of being frightened or disturbed by the violence, a coked-up Tiffany had laughed.

Melissa had killed no one but was the most shaken by the incident. That hadn't stopped her from noticing Tiffany's reaction. When it came time for her husband to be killed, Melissa wanted Tiffany to handle it. Tiffany had agreed to do it, for a bigger cut of the money.

"Do you see anyone following you?" Larry said on the phone.

"No," Tiffany said, "but if we're dealing with a pro like we think we are, I probably wouldn't spot him."

"How much longer until you get here?"

"A few minutes. Make sure Rudy is ready."

"He'll be ready, and he's armed too. Remember, Rudy is ex-army."

Tiffany smiled into the phone. "Three guns against one; I like those odds."

~

A few minutes later, Tanner watched Tiffany turn off the road and enter a driveway on the right. As he drove past, Tanner saw that the paved entrance was long and had a cracked surface. If there was a house beyond the curving path, it was too far back to be seen from where he was.

After driving around the next bend in the road, Tanner pulled over to the shoulder. He debated whether to travel back on foot or drive the rental. He decided to take the rental car. If someone saw him on foot, it would look like he was skulking about. If he simply drove onto the property and was caught or outnumbered, he could always claim to be a lost tourist.

Tanner had one weapon on his person and another hidden in the car. The weapon he was carrying was a small pocket pistol that only fired five rounds. The sniper rifle he'd used to kill Carl, the Jack Bellamy look-alike, had been dismantled and was sitting at the bottom of a nearby river.

Tanner thought the small gun would be enough for dealing with a group of con artists. After checking his mirrors, he pulled back onto the road, traveled a short distance, then made a U-turn.

A VICTIM OF CIRCUMSTANCE

~

"There's a car headed down the driveway," Rudy said into a phone. He was alerting Tiffany and Larry about Tanner's approach.

There was no house on the property, at least, not anymore. It had burned down during a fire caused by lightning a month earlier. The group knew about the property because they had scouted it when they were looking for a place to stash Bellamy.

Once the fire had left only burnt timbers behind, they had found another empty home to use. Such homes dotted the surrounding area. Byzantine had once boasted a factory that made automobile components. The parts plant moved its operations to Mexico several years earlier and took the jobs with it. Many of the larger homes in the area, whose owners were suddenly devoid of an income, were foreclosed on or abandoned.

Rudy was off on the side of the road and sitting behind the wheel of the small truck. He and Larry had spent time that morning using tarps with a camouflage pattern to help it to blend in with the trees. After they supplemented the tarps with branches of different sizes, the truck was hard to spot unless someone came close to it.

The truck was an old delivery van. It was the type that could be driven with the side door slid open for easy entering and exiting. A small space on the windshield had been left clear to use as a viewport, Rudy squinted as he tried to get a clear look at Tanner.

"It's one man. He's got dark hair and is wearing glasses. I think the car's a rental," Rudy said. "This might just be someone who got lost."

Larry was near the house. He was hidden behind a fallen tree that had been burnt by the fire, while Tiffany was tucked behind a small fence that was closer to the driveway. The plan was for Rudy to block the way out with the truck after Tanner entered. Afterward, Tiffany and Larry would shoot him down like a rabid dog.

"Whoever this is, I say we kill him," Tiffany said, "and I really hope it's the bastard who murdered Carl."

Rudy's whispered voice came over the phone. "Okay, guys, he's driving in now."

Tiffany took the safety off her gun, as Larry lowered himself behind the charred timber then used the burnt wood as a firing platform for the rifle he held. The Winchester was poised to take aim as Tanner drove onto the property. The trap was set, and the mouse had taken the bait.

6
MISTER X

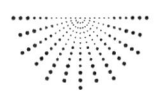

Jack Bellamy's lawyer and family friend Peter Fairfax studied Melissa as she spoke with the FBI agents. Fairfax had been a good friend of Bellamy's late father and had known Jack Bellamy since the day he was born. That said, he never liked the devious bastard, but he pretended to and had defended Bellamy publicly on many occasions. The association had proven to be a lucrative one for Fairfax, who handled all of Bellamy's legal work.

Fairfax was sixty-seven, lean, and gray-haired. His animosity for Jack Bellamy wasn't the only emotion he kept hidden. Peter Fairfax was infatuated with Melissa Bellamy to the point of obsession.

Although he had never revealed his true feelings for his client's young wife, Melissa was aware of the effect she had on Fairfax. To amuse herself, she sometimes teased Fairfax by invading his personal space, or bending forward when she was wearing a blouse with a low neckline.

What Melissa didn't know was that Fairfax had placed a hidden camera in her bedroom months earlier. The camera had given Fairfax more than a look at Melissa's naked body, it had also allowed him to discover her true nature.

It hadn't shocked him to learn that Melissa was sleeping with Bellamy's half-brother Sammy. After all, Sammy Bellamy was a nineteen-year-old blond Adonis. Fairfax could tell the affair meant no more than sex to Melissa and that she carried zero guilt over it. In the early stages of the relationship, the younger Bellamy often told Melissa that they had to stop seeing each other. Of course, he only said those words *after* they'd had sex.

"Why should we stop, Sammy? Don't you know that your brother cheats on me? Why shouldn't I have fun too?"

"It just feels wrong, Melissa."

"Oh really?" Melissa had said, as she disappeared beneath the covers. "And how does this feel?"

Eventually the young man stopped worrying and just enjoyed the ride.

Fairfax was thrilled whenever he watched the two of them together. Having a camera in Melissa's bedroom was like having a private porn website that only he knew about. He soon became aware that sex wasn't the only thing Melissa Bellamy wanted from her brother-in-law. She was grooming Sammy to be a co-conspirator in a kidnapping.

Rather than becoming disenchanted, Melissa's devious nature had aroused Fairfax and made him want her all the more. Staging a kidnapping to keep Jack Bellamy from filing for divorce was brilliant, given Bellamy's sadistic nature. Fairfax had warned him during his prior two marriages that he was tempting fate by waiting until the last moment to cut his wives off. The advice had fallen on deaf ears then.

Bellamy reveled in seeing the misery in the women's eyes when they realized they weren't getting any money out of the marriage after all.

With his last wife, Bellamy had actually staged a phony break-in, so that the woman's jewelry would go missing. Bellamy's third wife had been a twenty-five-year-old actress named Raina. She'd left the marriage with only memories, and a hatred for Jack Bellamy. When the insurance company finally paid the claim on the "stolen" jewelry, Bellamy kept the check.

Fairfax looked on in admiration as he watched Melissa play the worried and devoted wife. Along with the hidden camera in her bedroom, Fairfax had also placed several inside her car. There was also a remote tap on Melissa's phone. That last item had been installed by a client of Fairfax's who was an ex-computer hacker.

Peter Fairfax knew about Melissa's past and her grifter friends. He had discovered her dubious associates while checking into Melissa's history for Jack Bellamy. Melissa had no arrest record; however, it was clear that she lived above the lifestyle of the waitress she had presented herself to be.

Instead of warning Bellamy that he was marrying a suspected con artist, Fairfax had told him that Melissa was what she seemed. Had he warned Bellamy, Melissa would have gone away, and Fairfax couldn't have that.

Learning that the man named Carl had been murdered by someone mistaking him for Bellamy had concerned Fairfax. He worried that the kidnapping idea would be abandoned. He also didn't want Melissa getting hurt.

Her brilliant idea to use the corpse at the restaurant put the kidnapping back on track while giving everyone an alibi for the time that Jack Bellamy went missing. Everyone that is, except for Sammy, Sammy who would ultimately be the patsy for the crime.

Unlike the gullible Sammy, Fairfax knew that Melissa

had no intention of letting Bellamy live. The woman had to believe that she stood to gain more if her husband died. Her greed and desire for wealth wouldn't be sated by the three million she would be eligible for in two days.

Fairfax couldn't fault her logic in assuming that Bellamy might have left her something in his will. In fact, he had. Given how the kidnapping plan was set-up, the authorities would have a difficult time proving she was involved.

Yes, Melissa had every reason to believe her plan was going to work, and once Bellamy was out of the way, she would be a free woman. At that point, Peter Fairfax planned to reveal his true self to Melissa. Fairfax smiled. She'd never see it coming.

~

At the home where Jack Bellamy was being held captive, Sammy Bellamy was talking to him while disguising his voice. He was seated on a chair outside the closet Bellamy was locked in. Sammy had just informed Bellamy that someone had tried to kill him.

"Who would want to kill me?" Bellamy said.

"It might be one of those people you cheated years ago."

"I didn't cheat anyone. I was just... creative with the way I ran my hedge fund."

"All I know is that we had a guy pretending to be you and someone killed him, so, maybe you're better off in that closet for a few days."

"What should I call you? How about Mr. X?"

"No, and I shouldn't be talking to you."

"Listen, Mr. X, do you like gold?"

"Gold? Like jewelry?"

"I'm talking gold bars. Before I went and made a deal with the Feds years ago, I hid away over a hundred gold bars, and these are kilo-size bars I'm talking about."

"How much is that worth?"

"It's worth millions. I'll split it with you if you help me get out of here. What do you say?"

"You're trying to trick me?"

"I'm serious. Think about it."

"I'm going away now. I'm really not supposed to talk to you."

"Why not?"

"If the others found out they would be mad at me."

"About that, why are you stuck here while they're all out having a good time?"

"They'll be here soon. They said they had a problem to take care of."

"What sort of problem?"

"They're setting a trap for the man who killed our friend."

"No offense, but I hope they all kill each other."

"I guess you would feel that way."

"Gold, my friend, think about the gold."

"Millions?"

"Millions, my friend, millions in gold."

"I've got to go."

~

Inside the closet, Bellamy listened to Sammy's footsteps recede. After overturning the bucket again, he climbed up on it and went to work on the ceiling while trying to escape.

7
A CLOSE CALL

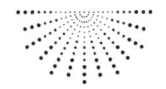

Tanner took one look at the burnt timbers of the house and knew he had driven into a trap. He brought his rental to a jarring stop, then yanked the shifter into reverse. Before the car could move back down the driveway, Rudy's truck exploded out of the trees and blocked Tanner's way.

Tanner lay flat across his vehicle's front seat while pressing his foot down harder on the gas pedal. A moment before the vehicle smashed into the side of Rudy's truck, there came a loud *CRACK!* and the car's windshield exploded.

Tanner registered that the round had been fired from a rifle, then he was jarred by the impact of hitting the truck. He was out of the vehicle an instant later and firing at the small truck. Much of the camouflage used to conceal it still clung to the vehicle, and Rudy remained unseen. Still, he was likely sitting behind the steering wheel; that was where Tanner aimed. He needed to remove the threat at his back.

The truck's windshield glass became a spiderweb of cracks after Tanner placed two rounds into it. Those rounds entered Rudy's torso, causing him to scream out in pain. Rudy collapsed and tumbled out the open door of the truck while clutching at his chest.

Shots pinged off the side of Tanner's rental even as the rifle boomed again. That meant there were at least two shooters. Tanner risked moving from behind the cover of the rear wheel to reach back into the car and grab the other gun he had with him. It was a Glock and loaded with eighteen rounds.

He raised his head above the level of the dashboard for an instant. Tanner caught a flash of blonde hair on his right and ten yards away. It was Tiffany, and she was moving in on his position.

Tanner ducked down again as a pair of shots from the rifle came. They destroyed more window glass and embedded themselves into the seat behind where Tanner's head had just been. More rifle shots ripped into the interior of the car causing Tanner to stay low.

The rental was still running and pressed against the truck while in reverse. Tanner shifted the gear lever into drive and turned the wheel toward the spot where he'd last seen Tiffany. The vehicle jerked forward, then slowed, but it continued moving.

Tanner heard Tiffany curse as she scrambled to avoid the vehicle. She must have been closing in on him while the rifle was keeping him pinned down. After slipping out of the car again, Tanner ran while bent low and made it to the driver's side of the truck where Rudy lay. The con artist turned kidnapper looked up at Tanner with glazed eyes as Tanner stepped over him.

Rudy had also been carrying a Glock. It lay on the floor of the truck with a splotch of Rudy's blood on it. The old truck had stalled when Rudy took his foot off the clutch. Tanner, while keeping low, restarted the vehicle and placed it in reverse. A new cry of agony escaped Rudy as Tanner ran over his ankles. The front wheels of the truck had to be angled so Tanner could turn it to face the street.

Bullet holes appeared, and glass shattered as Tanner was taking off. He remained low and used the open door to judge his proximity from the trees lining the edges of the driveway. When the truck listed to the right he understood that a rear tire had been destroyed by a rifle slug.

After going around a curve, Tanner sat up straight. The windshield was in thousands of pieces upon the floor and wind rushed past his face. He drove the limping vehicle while checking the one remaining side-view mirror for pursuit, but he saw none.

When an older couple in a Buick drove past him, they stared with wide eyes. A newspaper had been lying on the seat of the truck. With the wind blowing in freely, the newsprint swirled about and escaped the vehicle like a series of featureless kites.

Tanner abandoned the truck on the street four blocks away and headed into a stretch of trees on his left. He knew that beyond the acres of forest was the parking lot of a shopping center. The small gun was back in his hand, while his own Glock and the one taken from Rudy were tucked out of sight. Tanner stopped several times to listen for sounds of pursuit. There was nothing to hear but the chirps of birds and the shrill calls of cicadas.

He had underestimated his foes, something he rarely did. They might be a gang of grifters and con artists, but they were no less deadly for it. Tiffany's participation in the ambush surprised him most of all. Tanner had taken her for a roper, which in con-speak meant she was the one chosen to gain Jack Bellamy's trust. Tiffany had used sex to get Bellamy alone, so he could be kidnapped. But Tiffany was more than eye candy and bait. Had she gotten close enough to do so, Tanner had no doubt she would have killed him.

After reaching the parking lot of the shopping center, Tanner stole a car after switching its license plates with another vehicle. As he drove back toward his hotel, he thought about his next move. Melissa Bellamy, the target's wife, was likely involved in the fake kidnapping. She was also surrounded by FBI and law enforcement agents at her estate. She would remain in their care until her husband's kidnapping was settled.

No matter. She was the key to getting answers and finding her husband's body. Tanner decided he would have a talk with Melissa Bellamy, and the FBI be damned.

∽

Tiffany and Larry stared down at Rudy's dead form as rage welled up inside them. Rudy had succumbed to his wounds after Tanner rolled the truck over his ankles. It left Rudy's lower body canted at an odd angle.

"This shouldn't have happened. We had the guy trapped," Larry said.

"Whoever he is, he's a pro and deadly," Tiffany said. "If I had been a little closer that car might have run me over."

Larry looked around, then headed toward Tiffany's Mazda. "We have to get out of here. All that shooting might bring the cops."

"What about Rudy?"

"We'll have to leave him; it can't be helped."

Tiffany followed Larry, but then stopped, hung her head, and released a cry of angst.

"What's wrong?" Larry said.

"Rudy hid Carl's body last night. Do you know where he put it?"

"Shit. I don't know where he hid him. Damn it. This simple plan of Melissa's is turning into a mess."

Tiffany drove, and as they passed Rudy's body, a sigh escaped each of them.

"That could have been one of us," Larry said. "I think we need to bring in help to deal with this hit man."

"What sort of help?"

"I'm talking about Joe and Billy."

"Carl's cousins? Yes, they would be good, and they would love to get their hands on the man who killed Carl."

"They're the meanest bastards I know. Can you get in touch with them?"

"I can leave a message. I hope they get it soon and come here. Whoever killed Carl and Rudy is too dangerous to leave running around. If we're not careful, he'll ruin the whole plan."

"That won't happen, not once we send the FBI proof that we have Bellamy. When that news gets out, the hit man will wonder how Bellamy survived."

"You're right, and he might even go away, don't you think?"

Larry shook his head. "Not if he's as much a pro as we think he is. That will only make him want to kill Bellamy more. And to do that, he'll have to go through us."

"Then why don't we just kill Jack and be done with it?"

"We can't. Remember, he has to be alive for Melissa to be eligible for the money. Once that date passes, Bellamy's a dead man."

"Along with that brother of his. I know he's young, but Sammy must be a fool as well. Any idiot would see we're setting him up to take the fall for everything."

Larry laughed. "That kid is blinded by sex. Melissa has

him wrapped around her finger. Luckily for him, he won't be around to face the music. Bellamy will be dead, Sammy will be dead, and we'll all be rich."

"Not all of us," Tiffany said, as she shed a tear over her lost love, Carl Leffler.

8
WHAT GOES UP...

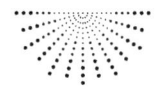

Jack Bellamy grunted as he skinned the knuckles on his right hand again. His kidnappers had left him a bucket to do his business in, but Bellamy was turning it into a tool to aid his escape.

The added height the bucket gave him when he turned it over and stood on it allowed him to reach the ceiling of the closet. All Bellamy had to do to gain his freedom was to break through a layer of plasterboard. Here too, the bucket came in handy, by providing a tool of sorts. Bellamy had removed the pail's metal handle and used its curled ends to gouge a hole.

On the other side of that barrier was a cramped attic. It wasn't much bigger than a crawl space, and to Bellamy's delight, no boards had been laid down across the floor joists, which had fiberglass insulation between them. Once he had the gap large enough, he could push aside a layer of insulation and pull himself up inside the attic.

After that, he would have a decision to make. To quietly escape without anyone noticing, or, find a weapon and seek revenge. Given his perverse nature, Jack Bellamy would relish vengeance above freedom. He thought about nothing else as he worked away at the plasterboard.

~

Tanner spotted the police vehicle parked in front of his hotel and wondered if it was there for him. As a precaution, he parked his stolen car a block away and hid his guns beneath the rear seat. His cover identity of real estate investor Paul Diehl was still intact, for now. On the ride back to the hotel, he had called and reported that his rental had been stolen.

Tanner doubted the police were at the hotel to see him about the car this soon, but it was best to be cautious. He had already met one bent cop in town and imagined the others wouldn't be much better. Having to stay in Byzantine longer than necessary was something else he owed the kidnappers.

Before entering the hotel, Tanner put his eyeglasses on again, so he would match the photo on his driver's license. A maid pointed him out to the cops the second he walked through the door. They approached him with suspicious eyes.

These two were older than the traffic cop Tanner had met upon first entering town. They also appeared more professional. One of them had a red nose, while his partner had a beer belly.

"Let's see your identification, buddy?" That order came from the cop with the red nose.

Tanner removed his wallet from a pocket and the cop with the beer belly snatched it from him.

"Up against the wall," said red nose, "I want to frisk you."

Tanner did as he said while asking, "What's going on?"

The cop ignored him while administering the frisk. There was a hidden razor blade at the rear of Tanner's belt and a shoelace was equipped with a handcuff key disguised as the lace's tip. Neither article had ever been detected before, and it remained so.

"He's clean, Eddie," red nose told beer belly.

"I'm here on business," Tanner said, "and I've done nothing wrong."

"Somebody has," said beer belly as he handed Tanner back his wallet. "Jack Bellamy was kidnapped last night. The chief told us to check out any strangers in town."

"Jack Bellamy? The guy involved in that hedge fund scandal? I saw that on the news, but I don't know anything about it."

The red-nosed cop stared at him coldly. "We've also had a spate of pockets getting picked lately. Do you know anything about that?"

"I'm no thief, Officer; I'm here to see about investing in local real estate."

The cop squinted at him with cold eyes. If it was an attempt to seem intimidating, it failed. Of course, given who he was dealing with, the cop could have pointed a Titan missile at him and Tanner wouldn't have been frightened.

After telling Tanner to "Watch his step," red nose and his partner beer belly left the hotel. When Tanner checked his wallet, he saw that it was a hundred dollars lighter.

∼

Jack Bellamy was grinning with glee as he pulled his feet up through the hole he had made in the ceiling. He was out of his cell but still far from free. He'd had to chin himself up to make it through the hole and the effort had winded him. He was seated on a floor joist with his legs spread out before him when he heard the car driving away from the house.

Only moments earlier he had listened to another vehicle arriving. Perhaps there was a shift change taking place. If so, Bellamy thought he'd be wise to get moving before someone checked on him.

The slanted attic ceiling caused him to have to walk bent over as he moved toward the door on the other side. The fiberglass insulation he'd touched made his hands itch. As he moved forward, he brushed his palms against the black slacks he wore.

The going was slow because he had to balance himself on a pair of two-inch wide joists. They were sixteen inches apart, and by having to stoop as he moved, it put strain on his knees. If he lost his footing, he'd likely step through the ceiling and keep going.

Bellamy had thought the closet was stuffy, but the temperature in the tight space of the attic was a dozen degrees hotter.

Thoughts of caution left Bellamy's mind when he heard a male voice drift up through the aperture he had made.

"Shit! There's a damn hole in the closet ceiling."

Bellamy quickened his pace. If he could make it out of the empty attic he might find something he could use as a weapon. He was nearing the door when his right foot slipped and sank into the pink insulation between joists.

Bellamy fell, landed on his butt, and felt pain at the base of his spine as he hit the unyielding wood of a joist. The plasterboard under the insulation had held, but when he placed pressure on it to stand, his foot pushed through.

The sound came of someone pounding up the staircase, causing Bellamy to panic. He yanked his foot from the hole, made it to his feet again, and moved as fast as he dared toward the door.

Gripping the knob, he prepared to meet whoever was on the other side of the door. It opened inward as if it had been kicked and the edge of the door hit Bellamy and sent him off-balance. He tumbled sideways, fell onto the insulation, and kept going.

The impact was hard as he hit the living room floor along with broken sections of plasterboard. If not for the cushion of insulation beneath him, Bellamy might have broken a bone. Nonetheless, he was dazed. By the time he opened his eyes to look around, Larry was coming back down the stairs, and he had a gun in his hand.

Bellamy looked him over and asked, "Are you Mister X?"

Seeing the blank expression on Larry's face, Bellamy knew he was right. There had been a shift change. When he noticed Tiffany, Bellamy moaned.

"You're part of this?"

"That's right, Jack."

"Damn, and I was thinking of making you my next wife."

"Keep an eye on him," Tiffany told Larry. "I'm going to get something to tie him up with."

After Tiffany disappeared into the kitchen, Bellamy sat up with a grunt, then smiled at Larry.

"Hey, do you like gold?"

9
TOP THIS

Joe and Billy Leffler had been hiring themselves out as muscle since they were teenagers. Presently in their thirties, they were experts at causing pain and making people disappear.

On the best of days, the brothers were ill-tempered. After finding out that their cousin Carl had been killed, Joe and Billy Leffler were in the mood to do some killing of their own. Fortunately for them, they had been paid to do just that to a man who had escaped going to prison for child molestation. The DNA evidence had been corrupted during a lab mix-up, and the victim was too traumatized to give a statement to the police. A first-hand account of the crime might not have revealed details anyway, given that the child, a boy, was only twenty-two-months-old.

The molester, who had been the janitor at a day care center, was thirty-seven-year-old Walter Hesburgh. Hesburgh was strapped down to an old wooden table. The Leffler brothers had grabbed him off the street and taken him to the basement of an abandoned apartment building.

The building, which was in Huntington, West Virginia, was slated for demolition, having reached the end of its fitness as a domicile. Still, Joe and Billy would put it to use one more time.

The brothers had received the news about their cousin as they were about to shoot Walter Hesburgh in the head. After learning about Carl, the Leffler brothers were ready to take out their anger on Hesburgh.

Before they'd strapped him to the table and gagged him, Hesburgh had sobbed and said how sorry he was.

He had confessed his sick crimes, then begged for mercy. Joe and Billy weren't capable of mercy and didn't care about Hesburgh or his twisted acts. They had been paid to kill him and make him disappear, and so they would.

Joe was the older brother by a year and two inches taller than Billy, who was six-foot-three. Joe was also smarter, which wasn't to say that he was by any means smart. Both men had dark hair, brown eyes, and faces like clenched fists. They wore plastic raincoats along with shower caps and gloves. When they were finished with Hesburgh, the raincoats, caps, and gloves would be burned.

It was Billy who'd started it. He had been about to shoot Walter in the temple when he thought about his dead cousin.

"Imagine if this was the guy that killed Carl. I'd give him one in the knee, like this."

Billy shot Hesburgh's right knee and the man released a howl of agony into the gag he wore.

"I'd do that too," Joe said, as he took out a knife. "But first, I'd gouge out his eyes."

When Joe went to work with the knife, Hesburgh forgot

all about the pain in his knee. By the time the brothers finished their game of, "This is what I'll do to the guy that killed Carl," Hesburgh resembled a failed experiment in Dr. Frankenstein's laboratory. Hesburgh had passed out less than a minute into the contest and died halfway through it.

"Look at the mess we made," Billy said.

"So what? We'll put the pieces in bags. They'll be easier to carry that way."

They went to work, but Joe was already thinking of their next task.

"Once we bury this guy we'll head to Byzantine and find the bastard that killed Carl."

"I can't wait to get my hands on him," Billy said, as he grabbed Hesburgh's severed head and tossed it in a trash bag.

∼

Melissa Bellamy smiled inwardly as she watched the two lead FBI agents take a white envelope from a uniformed cop. She already knew what was in the envelope and had been expecting its arrival.

"I think there's been a development," Peter Fairfax said. He was seated nearby and gesturing toward the agents.

"Do you think they've rescued Jack?"

"No, my guess would be that they've received proof he's alive. You know, like a photo showing him with a copy of this morning's newspaper."

Melissa's eyelids fluttered. That was exactly what was in the envelope. She was staring at Fairfax when the male, or no, the female, maybe it was the female agent? It was so damn hard to tell them apart. Anyway, one of the agents,

Williams or Willis, called to her and asked her to come over to where they were, in the foyer.

Melissa, wearing a modest skirt that fell below her knees, walked over to the agents with Fairfax following. When she saw the photo of Bellamy strapped to a chair with duct tape covering his mouth, she released the horrified gasp she had practiced for days.

"Oh my God. What have they done to him?"

"This is actually good news, Mrs. Bellamy," said one of the FBI agents, possibly the man. "We now have confirmation that your husband is alive and well. The kidnappers also reiterated that they want a million dollars."

"A million dollars? I don't, I mean, Jack's always handled our money. I don't know how to get hold of that much cash."

"I can help with that," Peter Fairfax said. As he spoke, he placed a hand on Melissa's arm.

The gesture was met with a look of surprise by Melissa. She was aware of Fairfax's interest in her, but the older man had never touched her before. When she looked over at him, Fairfax was smiling at her in a most peculiar way. As he removed his hand, he did so by sliding it down along her bare arm, as his fingers danced on her flesh. Afterward, Fairfax addressed the FBI.

"I'm not only Jack Bellamy's lawyer, Agent Williams, Agent Willis, I'm also a close family friend and advisor who has access to several of his accounts. I'll call the bank and arrange to have the money gathered."

As Fairfax and the agents huddled together to make plans for the transfer of the funds, Melissa returned to her place on the sofa. She didn't understand how he could possibly know anything, but she found herself wondering if Peter Fairfax was somehow on to her, and aware that she was part of the kidnapping.

How could he be? No, the old letch can't know a thing. I'm just being paranoid.

And yet, Melissa hadn't liked that smile of his, not one bit.

10
LET'S TALK

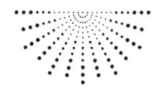

AFTER THE COPS LEFT, TANNER WENT UP TO HIS HOTEL room and wiped down every surface, eradicating his prints. The hotel, along with his identity of real estate developer Paul Diehl, had become a liability. He had less than twenty-four hours to find Bellamy's body and prove he had fulfilled the contract.

Those plans altered when Tanner was seconds from leaving. He had put the local news on as he wiped down the room and was amazed when a picture came on the screen.

It was the photo the FBI had shown Melissa, and Peter Fairfax. When Tanner saw Bellamy alive with a copy of the morning newspaper, he wondered what the hell was going on.

His first thought was that the kidnappers had created the picture using a photo manipulation tool. But no, they didn't strike him as being foolish enough to think something like that would deceive the FBI. That meant the photo was real.

For a brief instant, Tanner felt distress at the thought

he might have killed an innocent man in Bellamy's place. But Bellamy had no twin brother or look-alike siblings. Whoever the man was he had killed, they were a part of the kidnapping team, and so not an innocent.

That would also explain the gang's desire to see him dead. He had killed one of their own, a friend. No, more than a friend, at least for Tiffany. Tanner recalled the kiss she had given the man before she drove away from the bungalow.

Things were worse than Tanner had believed. Not only was his target hidden away somewhere and out of reach, but he had failed to fulfill the contract. It was no longer a case of gaining proof of his kill, but he still had to make good on the contract. He checked his watch. It was a little after one p.m., and he had until noon the next day to find Jack Bellamy and kill him.

Tanner left his hotel room. It was time to talk to Melissa Bellamy and get answers.

~

AT THE BELLAMY ESTATE, FBI SPECIAL AGENTS WILLIAMS and Willis were praising Chief of Police Martin Greene for his cooperative attitude.

"You might be surprised how often local law enforcement balks at our involvement," said Agent Willis.

"All I care about is getting Jack Bellamy back in one piece," the chief said. "I would call in the Marines if I thought they would come."

The Chief spoke the truth, although it was only because he had so much on the line. If Jack Bellamy wasn't found and freed, Chief Greene's secret would come to light within days. The chief imagined what it would be like if everyone knew the truth about him. If that were to happen, life as he knew it would end, and he'd have to leave town and start over.

The chief had grown up in Byzantine. The son of a carpenter, he'd been a cop since he was nineteen. His salary was small, but he made several times that amount from bribes and other illegal activities.

Byzantine was often cited as being a corrupt town with a questionable police force. Their critics were often silenced when it was pointed out that, per capita, they had one of the lowest crime rates in the country. Not that there weren't numerous crimes being committed every day, with a good portion of them being performed by his own cops. It's just that reporting said crimes was frowned upon, and most residents knew better than to do so.

Thinking of the town's crime statistics reminded the chief of another problem he had. There was a pickpocket operating in town, possibly even a team of them. Several people had reported that their wallets had been lifted. Chief Greene didn't give a damn about the pickpocketing itself. It angered him that he wasn't getting a cut of the action. Once the perp was found, some of the burlier cops on the force would have a talk with the thief and explain the facts of life to him. If you wanted to play in Byzantine, you had to pay.

As for the kidnappers, they would all get a bullet if the chief had his way. The anxiety they were causing him was brutal. He knew he wouldn't sleep at all until Bellamy was found.

But what if he isn't found in time and my secret comes out?

That thought caused the chief to shudder. No one could know his secret, no one. He would never live it down.

Inside her bedroom, Melissa Bellamy was using a burner phone to read and leave messages left in an email account's draft folder. Melissa's bedroom was just that, hers. She and Bellamy shared a bed often for sex, but Jack snored like a chainsaw at full throttle some nights. Separate bedrooms were preferred by Melissa anyway, and she was looking forward to having the entire house to herself once Jack was gone.

When she read the message from Tiffany about Rudy being killed by the hit man who was out to kill her husband, Melissa became worried. She felt better when she read on and learned that Joe and Billy Leffler were coming to town. Carl's cousins were a couple of psychos. Once they got their hands on the man who killed their cousin that threat would end.

Then, Melissa learned that Bellamy had seen Larry and Tiffany's faces. She smiled. What did it matter? Jack would be dead soon anyway.

There was a knock on the door. Melissa hid the phone beneath a pillow, put on her worried wife look, then opened the door. She had expected to see one of the androgynous FBI agents, instead it was her brother-in-law and lover, Sammy Bellamy.

Sammy tried to step inside the room, but Melissa pushed him back into the hallway. Didn't the fool realize they couldn't be alone in her bedroom with other people in the house? She walked briskly toward a side door and went outside. After strolling over to a gazebo, Melissa looked around, and seeing no one, she spoke to Sammy.

"Did the FBI question you?"

"Yeah, but I don't think they suspect me of anything."

"Jack broke out of that closet he was locked in."

"Oh crap, really? Did he see anyone's face?"

"He saw both Tiffany and Larry, but it doesn't matter, Sammy. They have alibis, remember?"

Sammy's young features clouded with worry. "About that, what happens when Jack hears about the night he was taken? Won't he realize he was never drunk in a parking lot?"

"Um, no," Melissa lied. "That drug he was injected with wiped out his memories of that time. He'll only know he woke up in that closet."

"I still don't like it that he saw Tiffany and Larry's faces. What if they decide it's too risky to leave Jack alive?"

"That won't happen, Sammy. At midnight tomorrow this will all be over, and Jack will be allowed to escape. Until then, we have to play along, especially you, since you'll be the one delivering the ransom money."

"Will I really be giving the money to someone?"

"We're going to make it look like the kidnappers got cold feet, remember?"

"Oh yeah. Too bad we can't keep it."

"I'll have three times that much once the clause in my prenuptial agreement kicks in, and you'll get a nice chunk of that."

Sammy raised a hand to caress Melissa's cheek and she took a step back to avoid it.

"Don't touch me when there are other people around."

"Sorry, but it's tough, you know. I just want to be with you all the time."

"Once this is over we'll spend some time alone, okay?"

The grin Sammy answered with made Melissa laugh. The mirth died in her throat when she noticed that someone was watching them from a window. It was the lawyer, Peter Fairfax, and he was wearing a grin of his own.

"Go back inside, Sammy. I don't want the FBI or the police wondering where you've gotten to."

"Are you coming in with me?"

"I'll return in a minute. It wouldn't look good if we came back in together."

Sammy walked off as Melissa gazed at the window where she'd seen Fairfax. The lawyer was no longer there. After concluding that Fairfax hadn't observed anything that might be seen as suspicious, Melissa left the gazebo.

She returned to the house through the same door she'd left it by and entered her bedroom again. She had no idea she wasn't alone until she was grabbed from behind and a hand clamped over her mouth. Then, a voice whispered in her ear.

"My name is Tanner. We need to talk."

11
HAVE YOU SEEN THIS GUY?

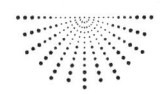

Joe and Billy Leffler met Tiffany in town at the same diner where Tanner had eaten the previous day. The waitresses/hookers took one look at the rough pair and decided that they would only offer the brothers what was on the menu. They instinctually knew that the Leffler brothers would like their play rough, perhaps too rough.

Tiffany declined food and sipped on coffee while the brothers devoured enough to satisfy four men. When they arrived, Joe had passed Tiffany a baggie containing cocaine in exchange for an envelope with cash in it.

Tiffany felt she would need the drug to get through the kidnapping. The truth was, she had needed the addictive stimulant for over a year and was hooked on it.

On the table between her and the brothers was a sketch she had made of Tanner. The likeness was good and showed Tanner wearing the glasses he sometimes wore. The spectacles had special lenses that tamed his fierce gaze.

"He looks like a hundred other guys," Joe said.

"I know," Tiffany said, "but he's in really good shape

and about six-feet tall. He has to be a stranger in town, so maybe that will help you find him."

"We made some calls on the way here and put out the word that we'll pay for information," Billy said. "In a town like this, anyone would finger the guy, even the cops. We'll get him."

Tiffany wiped away a tear. "If you take him alive I want a piece of him. I want to make the bastard suffer for killing Carl."

"Oh, don't you worry, baby, he'll suffer all right," Joe said.

"I want to know who hired him too. Whoever wanted Bellamy dead is responsible for the hitter being here in the first place."

Joe waved that idea away. "The hit man won't be able to give you a name. These guys don't deal directly like Billy and I do sometimes. That way he can't finger anybody if the cops get to him."

"What if the cops get to him first for something else?" Tiffany asked.

Billy laughed. "In this town? Hell, we could probably just buy the guy from them. There's a reason the mob doesn't operate in Byzantine; the cops got the place sewed up, and they can arrest the competition."

"I don't care how you do it, but get this guy and make him pay," Tiffany said.

"He'll pay all right," Joe said, "and in a small town like this, he won't be able to hide for long."

∽

TANNER WASN'T HIDING. HE HAD SNUCK PAST POLICE, reporters, and the FBI to enter the Bellamy home and find Melissa Bellamy. After grabbing his target's wife in her bedroom, he let her know that he was on to her scheme. At first, Melissa denied it, but then she realized that Tanner was hardly in a position to go to the police or the FBI.

"You killed the wrong man yesterday."

"I know that now. What I don't know is why your friend was made-up to look like your husband."

"Carl was pretending to be Jack so we could make it look like Jack was kidnapped later than he actually was."

"To establish alibis?"

"Yes."

"That's why you were toting that corpse around last night. I guess it worked."

Melissa put on a smile as she tried to ignore the knife Tanner was holding.

"We can both get what we want if we work together. I only need to keep Jack alive until midnight tomorrow so that a clause in our prenuptial agreement takes effect. After that, he's all yours."

"That won't work for me. I have a deadline that ends at noon tomorrow. I also know you and your group want revenge against me."

"Tiffany wants you dead, not me. She and Carl were close."

"If she or anyone else comes at me again, I'll kill them. If I don't find Bellamy before noon tomorrow, I'll come back here and kill you."

"Why kill me?"

"Because you and your grifters are in my way. If you want to keep living, tell me where I can find your husband."

"I... I don't know where they're keeping him."

"I don't believe you."

"No, it's true. The plan was to keep moving Jack around so that we don't draw attention by staying in one place too long. In a town like this people notice a group of strangers, so we picked several out of the way places to hide at."

"Then give me a list of those places."

"I can't. Tiffany is the only one who knows them all."

Tanner laid the edge of his knife against Melissa's throat. "It sounds like you're useless to me."

Melissa tilted her head back and spoke in a rush. "I can find out where they'll be later tonight. That way you can get there ahead of them."

Tanner removed the blade, but he kept the knife pointed at Melissa's stomach.

"I'll give you an email address. If I don't get word from you soon I'll be back."

"You'll hear from me. To hell with the kidnapping and Jack. I can't spend the money if I'm dead."

"Remember that," Tanner said.

After giving her an email address that Melissa could use to communicate with him, she assured Tanner she would make contact soon.

Without warning, Tanner grabbed Melissa, spun her around, and wrapped an arm about her neck. With his other hand, he pressed her head forward and shut off the blood flow to her brain. Melissa struggled in fear as a scream died in her throat. Eight seconds later she was unconscious, and Tanner let her drop forward onto her bed.

∾

MELISSA REGAINED HER SENSES MERE SECONDS LATER AS blood flow was resumed. Despite that, she was disoriented and felt unable to move for several moments. When she was able to shift her position, she did so in a rush as she looked around her bedroom in a panic.

She had seen someone knocked-out before in such a manner and understood what had happened. That knowledge helped to calm her, along with the fact that she had managed to buy herself more time. Walking into the bathroom, she lowered her head at the sink and splashed water onto her face.

Tanner would have to be handled. If not, he would kill her and everyone else involved. Melissa dried her face, then walked back into the bedroom to leave a message for Tiffany. She wanted to let the Leffler brothers know that they had to kill Tanner as soon as possible. When a better idea came to her, Melissa put the phone away and began laughing.

She had just thought of a way to rid herself of Tanner without placing any of her friends at risk. She would send a message to Tanner telling him where Jack Bellamy would be moved to. Bellamy wasn't being moved anywhere, although they did have a backup location.

No, Tanner would be all by himself once he reached the destination she would direct him to, but he wouldn't be alone for long. Melissa laughed aloud, caught herself, and again feigned looking distraught over the kidnapping of her beloved husband.

~

JOE AND BILLY CAUGHT A BREAK WHEN A MAID AT THE Byzantine Hotel recognized the sketch of Tanner that Tiffany had given them. She also recalled that he was going by the name of Paul Diehl. Their luck ran out when the woman didn't recall what room he was in.

No biggie, Joe thought. They could get his room number

and other information from the guy manning the front desk.

The assistant hotel manager on duty was a young man named Kurt Dobson. Kurt was dressed in a suit and tie, wore polished shoes, and was knowledgeable about sites of interest and historic value in the Byzantine area. The twenty-five-year-old spoke three languages, was a college graduate, and possibly the town's only honest citizen.

When Joe and Billy asked him for information about Tanner, Kurt sent them a glare of reproach.

"Gentlemen, it is against the hotel's policy to give out such details concerning our guests."

A crooked smile parted Joe's lips as he reached into a pocket and took out his wallet. A twenty-dollar bill was flung onto the counter.

"Does that change your policy?"

Kurt was appalled as he looked down at the crumpled bill. "Are you attempting to bribe me?"

Billy's patience, which was thin on a good day, had neared its end. He moved around the counter and grabbed Kurt by his paisley tie.

"If you don't tell us what we want to know you'll be spitting up teeth."

"He's, he's, he's gone... checked out," Kurt said.

"Any forwarding address?" Joe asked.

"No, but I heard that he had his rental car stolen. Perhaps he'll be at the agency down the street looking to rent another vehicle."

Joe scooped up the twenty as he spoke. "Let's see the form he filled out to check in."

Kurt slid the registry across the desk, and Joe ripped out the sheet that had Tanner's information on it. Billy released Kurt, only to give him a hard slap across the face.

That caused the young man to cry, and Joe and Billy chuckled at his tears.

When the brothers left the hotel, Kurt grabbed the phone off the desk and called the police. He was going to report the incident to Chief Greene himself.

12
MILLIONS IN GOLD

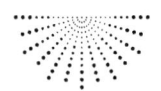

There was a flurry of activity at the Bellamy estate when a cop delivered a large envelope from the kidnappers. The envelope had been tossed through the open window of a police car while the cop was inside a fast food restaurant responding to a disturbance.

The police officer had opened the envelope and found a cell phone and a note. He read the note, then called Chief Greene. There was a single sheet of paper giving instructions about how and when the ransom drop would go down. Sammy Bellamy was to be the one who would bring the ransom.

The letter warned that there was to be no attempt made to follow Sammy or to place a tracking device in with the cash. If either of those things occurred, Jack Bellamy would pay for it.

Of course, the FBI and the police would ignore both of those warnings. Grabbing a kidnapper at the drop-off point for the ransom was their best bet at getting Bellamy back safely. Sammy was handed-off to FBI specialists that would make certain he could be tracked no matter what the kidnappers put him through.

The current generation of tracking devices were waterproof, non-jammable, and undetectable by anything other than an extreme search of their wearer's person. The device could pick up sound within a thirty-foot radius and contained an HD camera.

As Sammy was being prepared, the federal agents were also gearing up, and a helicopter with infrared was on standby. Seeing all of the effort being employed to return Jack Bellamy gave Chief Greene hope that his secret would remain safe. He also had new leads to follow.

There had been the complaint call made from Kurt at the hotel. It seemed that some muscle types were in Byzantine looking for a man named Paul Diehl. Diehl had been questioned along with every other stranger in town. Unlike the others, Diehl's rental car had been discovered at the site of a homicide, and the man himself had disappeared.

Whether he had anything to do with the kidnappers was unknown. The same could be said for Jack Bellamy's latest conquest, a young woman named Tiffany.

The chief had received a tip from a bartender that Bellamy had been cheating on his wife again. That was not surprising, given that Bellamy had the morals of a pig. Still, even if the young woman wasn't involved with the kidnapping, perhaps she might know something useful.

The chief decided he would look into both leads personally if the ransom drop didn't produce anything. One way or another, Jack Bellamy had to be found.

Peter Fairfax sidled up beside Melissa as she stood leaning in a doorway. When she turned to look at Fairfax, Melissa saw that he was smiling in contentment.

"What are you so happy about, Peter?"

"The ransom drop of course. In a few hours Jack could be back home. Isn't that wonderful?"

"I know you don't like him."

"Pardon me?"

"Don't deny it. I've seen how you look at him sometimes when he doesn't know you're watching him."

"I don't know what you're talking about, Melissa. Why, that would be as ridiculous as believing you only married Jack for his money. By the way, I believe you're closing in on one of the terms stated in your prenuptial agreement, isn't that correct?"

"I can't even think about money at a time like this."

Fairfax chuckled. "Melissa, my dear, you rarely think about anything else."

Melissa removed her shoulder from the doorway and turned to stare Fairfax in the eye.

"Are you accusing me of something, old man?"

"No, and I think you know I am an admirer of yours. If I've said anything to offend you, I apologize."

Melissa stared at Fairfax a little longer, then turned away when she was summoned by one of the FBI agents.

"Mrs. Bellamy, ma'am, could you come here, please?"

"Of course," Melissa said.

As she was walking away, Melissa glanced over her shoulder. That's when she saw that Fairfax was wearing that damn smile again, the one that said he knew something. That smile made her nervous.

∼

At the secluded home where Bellamy was being held, Larry was keeping an eye on the man while Tiffany ran out to get food.

Since they were no longer able to use the closet for a cell, Larry came up with the idea of wrapping chain around Bellamy's ankles. The chain was secured by a padlock, while its other end was fastened around the metal frame of the recliner he sat in.

When it was time for Bellamy to use the bathroom, the chain could be extended by removing several other padlocks that kept the chain from stretching out to its full thirty feet of length. The padlocks were keyed alike, so only one key was required to unlock them. If Bellamy tried to escape, he'd have to bring the heavy recliner along with him.

This set-up allowed Bellamy the freedom to avoid confinement in a closet, while the rattle of the chain alerted Tiffany and Larry whenever he so much as twitched. Tiffany was opposed to the idea until Larry pointed out an added benefit. If Bellamy was mobile, he could use the bathroom and they wouldn't have to empty his poop bucket. Hearing that, Tiffany became a fan of the chain idea.

Larry had agreed to let Bellamy have a can of beer. The two sat drinking the brew while watching a baseball game on TV. During a commercial break, Jack Bellamy looked around at the house while shaking his head.

"Why are there so many holes in the walls?"

"Don't worry about it," Larry told him.

The house they were using was foreclosed on months earlier and had been sitting vacant ever since. Before leaving the home, its former owners went about with sledge hammers and knocked holes in most of the walls. It had been their dream home and a secluded oasis.

Someone should have told them that banks could be less than understanding when you failed to pay your mortgage.

The area had seen many homes wind up in foreclosure since the factory closed, and the bank would eventually get around to repairing the house and placing it on the market. When they did, they would also need to mend the openings Bellamy had made in the ceiling.

The TV was still showing commercials. When Bellamy reached out for the remote, Larry went for the gun on his hip.

"Whoa, calm down," Bellamy said. "I just want to mute the TV."

"Why?"

"I want to talk. I have an offer for you."

"What sort of offer?"

"You let me go free and I'll tell you where I've hidden millions in gold."

"Millions?"

"That's right."

"Bullshit!"

"The gold is real. It's like a sort of insurance I have. If everything ever turned to total shit, I wanted to make sure I wouldn't be broke again. Years ago, when I first got mega-rich, I buried over a million in gold. It's gone way up in value since then."

Larry's eyebrows arched. "It must be at that big house of yours."

"It's not even in this state. I buried it back when I was living in New York City."

"You're saying you buried gold in New York City?"

"Not in the city, but near it. I still own property there."

Larry appeared as if he were giving the idea serious consideration, but then he shook his head.

"Even if you were telling the truth, how would I know it?"

"Easy. Keep me locked up while you go get the gold. Once you get the gold, call the cops and tell them where to find me."

Larry rubbed a hand over his chin. "That could work."

"Hell yeah it would, and we'd both get what we want. I'd be free, and you'd be rich."

"I'd have to share it with my partners."

"Like that bitch Tiffany? You see what trusting her has gotten me. Once she had the gold she'd shoot you in the back."

"She's not like that."

"Tiffany is a coke whore. You can't trust a coke whore."

"She'd never try to hurt me."

"She's also never seen that much gold before."

Larry rubbed his chin again, as greed ate its way into his mind.

"Gold," Bellamy said, his voice a melodious whisper. "Millions in gold."

13
RANSOM DROP

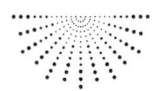

Tanner was beginning to think he'd have to pay Melissa Bellamy another visit when he received an email message from her.

It was an address in Byzantine that Bellamy would be moved to. There wasn't a doubt in Tanner's mind that Melissa was sending him into a trap. That was fine by Tanner. It would give him a chance to grab one of the kidnappers and make them talk. If Melissa hadn't been within shouting distance of a dozen cops and federal agents, Tanner would have made her reveal Bellamy's location.

The email stated that Bellamy would be moved to a certain house in the late evening. Tanner would head there as soon as possible and prepare. With that in mind, he went to gather supplies.

As he was driving toward a shopping center along the town's main drag he stopped at a traffic light. While glancing around, Tanner spotted the little girl he'd seen earlier. Her blonde curls glistened in the sun as she stared up into the branches of a tree. It seemed her kitten had gotten away from her again.

The child spoke to a man walking by as she pointed up into the trees' lower branches. As the light changed, Tanner saw the man put down the grocery bag he'd been lugging along and reach up into the tree for the cat. The girl was nearly as young as the kitten. As Tanner drove away, he wondered where her parents were.

~

THE SHOPPING CENTER HAD AN OFFICE SUPPLY STORE. Tanner made most of his purchases there as he gathered large cardboard boxes, string, spray-on glue, and black and silver spray paint. A sports shop provided him a dark, lightweight jogging outfit and a matching backpack, along with every hand warmer they had in the store.

The last item, the hand warmers, had to be dug out of a back storeroom, since it was spring. They were the type that came in foil pouches and produced heat for hours due to a chemical reaction.

Tanner was wearing a cap with a long bill to help block the view of cameras. His sunglasses were dark and hid his eyes well. His preparations might remain unneeded. If not, they would be used, and could make the difference between death and survival. He paid for everything with cash and was careful not to leave behind a fingerprint.

~

THE RANSOM MONEY ARRIVED FROM THE BANK INSIDE AN armored car. After verifying the funds were all there, and in the denominations demanded in the ransom note, it was time for Sammy to leave.

A VICTIM OF CIRCUMSTANCE

The surveillance device Sammy Bellamy carried on his person was the size of a dot and resembled a mole. It was affixed to his body at a spot beneath his chin and would stay attached unless he was sand-blasted.

The bills comprising the ransom had been sprayed with an odorless, colorless chemical that could only be detected under a certain spectrum of infrared light. If the money somehow made it into circulation, the FBI would be able to trace where and when it was spent. In a previous case of kidnapping, the perpetrators were caught after the marked bills were tracked back to them.

It was expected that Sammy would be made to move about the area in a circuitous and chaotic manner in an attempt to lose anyone following him. However, there was no need to tail the young man. As long as his "mole" stayed attached, the FBI would have him under total surveillance.

The lead agents, Williams and Willis, had called in other agents from the surrounding area to assist. In all, there were twenty-two men and women. Supplementing that force were eight of Chief Greene's men.

Melissa took in the impressive effort and technology going into locating and rescuing her husband. She was glad she and the others had the good sense not to attempt to claim the ransom. She had known most kidnappers were caught at that stage of their crime, now she knew why it was true. Anyone found near that money would have no chance of escaping from the scene. If they resisted arrest or appeared hostile, they would be cut down before they took their next breath.

Sammy sent Melissa a nervous glance, accepted a pat on the shoulder from Chief Greene, then headed out the door. He was going to play his final part in Melissa's kidnapping scheme. And after that, Sammy's usefulness would be at an end.

～

THE HOUSE WHERE MELISSA SENT TANNER WAS BUILT TO look like a log cabin. The effect worked from a distance, but once you got closer you could see that the logs weren't real. It was a large home and appeared to be about a decade old. Its shuttered windows, along with the high grass of its lawn, spoke of it having been closed up for months.

It was surrounded on all sides by thousands of trees interspersed with small streams. The road that granted access to it was at its northern end. A long driveway snaked from the road to a graveled parking area. Tanner was wearing all black after having changed in the car.

He had approached the house from the east while traveling on foot. He ignored the home. Although it appeared to be an ideal location to stash a kidnap victim, Bellamy would never be in that house. Melissa Bellamy must have expected Tanner to break into the home and lie in wait, if so, he would disappoint her.

His goal was to take one of the kidnappers alive and make them lead him to his target. He had less than eighteen hours to complete the hit on Bellamy, and a Tanner never failed. He went to work readying himself for a confrontation, as the hours ticked away.

14

DIVIDE AND CONQUER

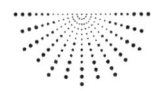

Tiffany had returned to the kidnapper's lair with enough food to last them a week.

After eating dinner, Larry entered a back room where he couldn't be overheard by Bellamy. It was time for him to go into action as the man who would put Sammy through his paces. Burner phones had been placed at different locations along with notes of instruction on what to do next.

Larry had his own set of phones along with a script he was to follow, while his voice would be electronically disguised. The plan was to keep Sammy on the move for hours, as if the kidnappers were making certain he wasn't being followed.

During that time, Sammy would be forced to strip out of his own clothes, swim underwater, change into a provided jumpsuit, then ride several buses. At a certain point he would be instructed to walk into a forest. Under a canopy of trees in full bloom, he would be hidden from any eyes in the sky the FBI might have.

Larry was looking forward to playing his part. He

didn't like Sammy. The kid had sold-out his brother while screwing the guy's wife. He and the others were professional con artists. Tricking and using people was their stock in trade, but Sammy, Sammy was just a louse.

When it came time to get rid of Sammy, Larry hoped he'd be the one to do it. Larry had almost told Jack Bellamy about his brother's betrayal, but then he figured, why bother? Both men would be dead soon.

Bellamy's talk of gold was bullshit. Larry knew that. Then again, a guy like Bellamy just might bury millions in gold as insurance. If not for his partners, Larry would have locked Bellamy up somewhere and went off on a treasure hunt in New York. Why not? If the gold was there, he'd be rich. If it was all a lie, he'd only be out airfare and the price of a shovel.

Larry considered telling Tiffany about the gold. If they worked together, she could keep an eye on Bellamy while he traveled to New York to look for the gold. But Tiffany would never go for that. She would be afraid that if Larry found the treasure he would keep it to himself, or simply deny finding it at all. He would feel the same way about letting Tiffany go off on her own.

Larry put on a set of headphones, opened a laptop, and accessed the software that could alter his voice. It was time to play the ransom drop game with Sammy. As he dialed the phone they had provided with the ransom note, Larry's mind was on gold.

∞

"How much gold?" Tiffany asked.

"Millions," Bellamy said.

He had told Tiffany the same tale he'd told Larry, and like her partner, Tiffany's eyes grew bright with greed. She and Bellamy were in the living room with the TV muted. He had noticed that she had a residue of white powder on her top lip, and she had moved about the kitchen in a frantic manner while cooking.

That was good. Cocaine users were known to become paranoid. Paranoia was something Bellamy could use to turn Tiffany against her partners. Then again, old-fashioned greed would likely be enough.

"How deep is the gold buried?"

"About as deep as a grave. It took me hours to bury it all."

"How much does a hundred kilos of gold weigh? I mean in pounds."

"Over two hundred pounds, plus the weight of the packing material and small crates I buried it in."

"And you did this when?"

"Back in 2002 I had just made a deal that netted me thirty million dollars. Had the deal gone the other way, I would have been in the hole for half that. That was when I decided to buy a million in gold for insurance. Once I had it, I felt free to take even bigger risks. It's one of the reasons I'm as rich as I am. No matter what happened, I knew I still had money to start over."

Tiffany took out her phone and searched gold prices, both the current price, and the price in 2002. Her eyes glittered when she saw what the current value of the gold would be.

"That's a lot of money," she whispered.

Bellamy smiled at her. "It can all be yours."

Tiffany grinned back at him. "I could torture you for the location."

"Try that, and I'll lie."

"You would give up the location eventually just to make the pain stop."

"Or I might keep lying out of pure spite and watch you traipse back and forth to New York State."

"I wouldn't have to go back and forth. Larry could torture you while I look for the gold."

Bellamy laughed. "Larry does the hard part while you get the gold, huh? You must think he's stupid. Once you had the right location you would tell him I lied again."

"I wouldn't do that. I would share it."

"And I would swear to him I gave you the real location and that you were playing him for a sucker. Larry might torture you next."

Tiffany thought it over and realized that Bellamy was right. Unless they went looking for the gold together, she and Larry would never trust each other.

"You're an evil bastard, Jack."

"And you're a conniving slut. What's your point?"

"There is no gold. You're lying."

"It exists, and I'll trade it to you for my freedom."

"Then you'll tell the FBI all about me."

"Did you give me your real name?"

"Of course not."

"Does anyone know your real name?"

"I began using the name Tiffany Hayes when I ran away from home at fifteen. No one knows my real name."

"And are your prints on file anywhere?"

"I've never been arrested even once," Tiffany said with pride.

"Then you have nothing to worry about, and with millions in gold you can get far away."

Tiffany's tongue ran over her lips, wetting them. Bellamy thought she looked like someone on the verge of devouring a great meal.

"Think of all the things you could do with that much money," Bellamy said.

"I am. With that much wealth, I could go anywhere, and I could be anyone I wanted to be. I'd be free."

"Gold," Bellamy said, his voice once again a melodious whisper. "Millions in gold."

∽

OUTSIDE THE HOME, JOE AND BILLY LEFFLER WERE peering through a narrow space between a window frame and the blind covering it. Joe had spotted Tiffany at a traffic light and decided to follow her. Once they had her location, they waited for a while before leaving their vehicle to check out the house.

Carl had told his cousins that he was coming into some big bucks soon, but he hadn't mentioned the kidnapping. Tiffany had to speak of it to explain to the brothers why Carl had been killed, and the million-dollar ransom had made them want to know more.

They left the window and moved quietly along the side of the house until they reached the rear. Moonlight revealed a deep hole that resembled a grave.

"They're not planning to send that guy home alive," Joe whispered as he pointed at the hole.

Billy nodded his agreement.

They kept walking and stayed to the edge of the trees until they were back at their car.

"Are we cutting ourselves in on that action, Joe?"

"We'll show up once they get the money. I see no reason why we shouldn't get Carl's cut."

"It's only fair, but what if they don't see it our way?"

"I like Tiffany, but she was Carl's girl, and Carl's dead. So yeah, I could kill her if it comes to that."

"Works for me," Billy said.

15
DROP YOUR WEAPON!

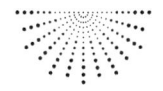

Tanner had been waiting for about an hour after having finished making his preparations. The moon was three-quarters full without a cloud in the sky. It illuminated the house, but beneath the thick cover of the trees, all was dark.

The wait ended when Tanner heard someone come trampling through the trees. That was followed by the beam of a flashlight appearing a short distance from where he was standing.

He hadn't seen or heard a vehicle and the nearest main road was over a mile away. If the approaching figure was sent there to kill him, he wasn't being stealthy about it. When the man came into view, Tanner saw that he was a young blond guy, tall, with a strong build. There was something familiar about him. However, with his face moving in and out of shadows beneath the trees, it was difficult to get a good look at him.

The kid resembled a college freshman. He had a linebacker's build and a child's face. He was also nervous and looked around with wide blue eyes. There was something bulky in his hands that appeared to be a laptop case or a satchel. There was no weapon in sight and no sign that he had been accompanied by an accomplice.

The boy stepped from the edge of the trees and into the moonlight, then walked over to the house and took a seat on the front steps. He just sat there, clutching that satchel, and looking like a kid waiting for his mom to pick him up.

When Tanner realized he was Bellamy's half-brother Sammy, he knew what must be in the satchel and that he'd walked into a greater trap than expected. There was ransom money in the case the kid held, and that meant the FBI was moving in from all directions.

He considered rushing at the boy and making him talk. If the wife was involved, perhaps Bellamy's brother was as well. Despite the potential benefit of learning where Bellamy was being held, getting such information from Sammy could cost Tanner dearly. It would take up valuable time that was best used to escape the area. Tanner moved deeper into the surrounding trees, as the FBI closed in.

~

A SHORT DISTANCE AWAY FROM THE HOUSE WERE THE offices of the security company that watched over the property. When Sammy Bellamy walked over to sit on the porch steps he had triggered a silent alarm.

Hal Hanson, a security guard, was on duty. Hal paused from playing a video game when the alert sounded.

He had been a Marine for four years in wartime and did little more than file away folders in North Carolina. When Hanson got discharged, he joined a city police force, and again, he was given the duty of working in the office.

The few times he was out on the streets were as boring as being inside. After acting in a manner that his captain termed too aggressive, during a routine traffic stop, Hal knew he would never be placed back in a patrol car again. In fact, they had told him he was lucky to keep his job at all.

That luck didn't hold. While off-duty, Hal beat up a man who he'd caught stealing a candy bar. After the man threatened to sue, Hal was kicked off the force.

When a buddy of his back home in Byzantine got him a job as a security guard with a property management firm, Hal expected more boredom. To his surprise, there was plenty of action, and without all the rules and paperwork he'd been burdened by during his time as a cop.

On his first week on the job he'd caught a junkie trying to break into one of the houses he protected. Hal had shattered a bone in the man's arm with a baton, causing the thief to run off into the woods while screaming in pain. The burglary tools left behind were proof that Hal had prevented a robbery, and his boss was pleased with him.

In the eight months since Hal started the job, he'd stopped six break-ins, rousted two groups of squatters, and turned in a man poaching deer. Hal had also gained a new partner named Denny. Denny was even more gung-ho than Hal and loved action. Denny was getting some action in a garage area from a female he'd met less than an hour earlier.

Hal had to admit that Denny had a way with the ladies. It wouldn't surprise Hal to find a bunch of little Denny's running around the area in the coming years.

Hal called to him through the open bay door. "Leave the bitch alone and get in the car. We've got a break-in to roll on."

Denny ignored Hal and kept... doing what he was

doing. When the act ended, Denny left his paramour and trudged over to the security patrol car. It was a Chevy Tahoe. Its markings made it resemble a police vehicle, complete with a light bar and an old-fashioned whip antenna.

"C'mon, Denny, we've got a perp to teach a lesson to."

Denny settled his nearly two-hundred pounds into the shotgun seat and Hal drove off toward the home where Sammy was waiting with the ransom.

∽

"MOVE IN! MOVE IN!" THAT SHOUTED COMMAND WAS SENT to the FBI agents surrounding the property where the ransom drop was going down. The sensitive listening device Sammy wore detected the sounds of movement within its range. That meant someone had been within thirty feet of Sammy Bellamy.

Of the twenty-two personnel working the kidnapping case, eighteen were field agents, and not tech support. Those fifteen men and three women were closing in from all sides on the home. They were equipped with thermal imaging monoculars and could detect each other because of the special headbands they wore. The bands emitted a pulsating heat signature that flashed twice every second. Only someone equipped with a thermal monocular would detect the signal.

Tanner had no such signal, while his body was giving off heat that was easily distinguished from his surroundings. He ran through the woods and hoped his precautions would be enough to keep him from being captured.

∽

A VICTIM OF CIRCUMSTANCE

FBI Agent Lissette Rivera was a rising young star in the Bureau. She intended to boost her career further by capturing the kidnapper under pursuit. Her heart rate took a jump when she spotted a figure standing fifty feet away. It was just a glowing man-size shape in her monocular and it appeared to be aiming a rifle at something on its right. Agent Rivera looked in that direction and saw a thermal flash. That meant a fellow agent was approaching and was in danger of being shot.

"FBI!" Agent Rivera shouted. "Drop your weapon!"

When there was no response, Agent Rivera didn't hesitate. She fired her Glock model 23 twice. Through the light of her monocular, it appeared as if her target's midsection had erupted. Oddly enough, despite leaning to the left, the suspect stayed on his feet and kept the rifle raised.

More shots sounded off from the other agent who had been approaching, and this time the target fell. The second agent closed in first, and Rivera heard her colleague let out a string of invectives. When Rivera reached the scene and saw what the other agent's flashlight beam revealed, she also cursed.

Lying on the ground was a cardboard cut-out made to resemble a rifle-wielding man. Splattered on it and the surrounding ground cover was the liquid from the numerous hand warmers used to give off a thermal signature.

More shouts of warning came from every direction, followed by other agents firing at additional targets that seemingly refused to drop their weapons. As Rivera shook her head in disgust, the communication channel flooded with urgent voices.

Some agents had encountered the phony targets, while others had set off unnoticed tripwires. The wires sent branches moving in a pattern, as if someone nearby were running away from, or toward them. The confusion ended when Special Agent Williams spoke and told everyone to calm down and remain cautious, but not to worry. A suspect was being pursued by the team with the tracking dog.

"No cardboard cut-out will fool that animal," Williams said.

~

TANNER WAS APPROACHING THE BACK ROAD WHERE HE'D left his car. He thought he had avoided the trap when he heard shouts being directed toward him from two men. They were doubtless telling him to surrender, but Tanner had other plans, like staying free.

His speed, combined with a weaving route through the trees which he had marked earlier, left the men behind and unsure of what direction he had taken. Above the trees there hovered a helicopter; however, it was back by the house illuminating the area with a searchlight.

Although nearly a mile distant, the chopper's noise masked the sound of the dog pursuing Tanner. He wasn't aware of the hound until it was closing in on him. Tanner looked over his shoulder. He saw glowing eyes and the glint of sharp teeth, as a massive German shepherd ate up the ground between them.

~

HAL BROUGHT THE SECURITY VEHICLE TO A SKIDDING STOP near the spot where Tanner's stolen car was hidden off-road. He'd been listening on a scanner and knew that a kidnapper was headed his way. If he and Denny caught the guy, their pictures would be in every paper in the country.

"Let's go, Denny!"

Denny was faster, bigger, and meaner than Hal, he was out of the SUV and headed toward Tanner. Hal laughed as he watched his partner. The look on Denny's face told him that he was out for blood.

∼

As the German shepherd grew closer, Tanner skidded to a stop, turned around, and raised his hands up at shoulder level. Dogs trained for law-enforcement are taught to fight you only as long as you combat them. If you stop and surrender, the dog is conditioned not to bite you. Instead, he will bark to hold you in place until his handler arrives. This dog was no different. Although he flashed his teeth and growled between barks, he made no move to take a bite out of Tanner.

Far from surrendering to the hound, Tanner was preparing to strike first. In his right hand he held what appeared to be a pen. It was actually a weapon that contained a powerful pepper spray. Tanner shifted the tip of the pen so that it was pointing at the dog's face, but before he could press the trigger, Denny came rushing up on him from behind.

∼

Chief of Police Greene kicked open the back door of the faux log cabin home and aimed his gun and flashlight around. The place was empty and unused. He could feel it, although he'd hoped to find Jack Bellamy inside. After the beam of his light revealed the junction box that controlled the home's propane generator, Greene activated it and turned on lights.

Sheets were draped over the sofas in the living room and the refrigerator was empty and smelled stale. Greene pulled out a kitchen chair, plopped into it, and for the first time considered what he would do if Bellamy wasn't found soon. Whatever new life he began, he would need money to finance it, and the chief knew right where to get it.

~

TANNER SPUN LEFT TO AVOID DENNY'S CHARGE THEN SAW that he wasn't the target of it. Denny, a Great Dane, had been going after Lobo, the FBI tracker dog, who'd had the temerity to be on Denny's turf. The bitch Denny had been humping back at the security headquarters was just that, a bitch, of the Rottweiler variety. The dog was in heat and Denny saw Lobo as competition for her. The two dogs went at each other ferociously, granting Tanner an opportunity to head for his vehicle again.

He was a hundred feet from the back road when he saw Hal's security patrol vehicle. Then, he spotted Hal, as the security guard jumped out from behind a tree.

Tanner had smelled his aftershave and heard his movements before Hal came into view. He squirted him with the pepper spray as Hal was bringing up his gun. The gung-ho guard released a wail, then had trouble catching a breath, as his eyes began to sting. Tanner guided Hal close to the security patrol vehicle and activated the light bar on the roof. Seconds later, the helicopter made a pass overhead. The metal bird had gone out in a wide circle and was searching for civilian vehicles.

From the air, Tanner and Hal would look like a team of cops guarding a perimeter position. When the chopper moved away, Tanner left Hal, who was still suffering from the pepper spray. After turning the vehicle around, Tanner drove off. If the helicopter spotted him again, it would mistake him for one of several patrol cars in the area.

The killing of Jack Bellamy had seemed an easy task to Tanner. Now, he had nearly died in an ambush, came close to being in the FBI's custody, and had only hours left before he became the first Tanner to ever fail. He swore to himself that when he finally left Byzantine behind him, that he would never return, not for all the money in the world.

16
SELF-INTEREST

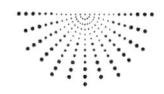

After the FBI failed to capture one of the kidnappers, Chief Greene decided to track down another lead. Bellamy was seeing a young blonde in the days before he went missing. Greene wanted to find out who she was.

The bald bartender inside the Byzantine Lounge recognized the chief and handed him his favorite drink as he approached the bar. There wasn't much of a crowd. If the lounge didn't supplement its income by selling drugs they would have closed years ago.

"There you go, Chief, a rum & coke."

The drink was pure Jamaican rum, while the coke, cocaine, came wrapped inside a small foil packet. Chief Greene slid the drug into an inside pocket before taking a sip of his drink.

"Hey, Chief, how come you never wear a uniform?"

"They make me look fat, Harry."

"You're here about that girl I told you about, right?"

"Have you seen her again?"

"No, but I can show you what she looks like," Harry said, as he pointed above the bar. "There's a camera up there that's aimed at the cash register. That girl you're looking for got into camera range the other night. We have her on video."

"Let me see it," the chief said, then he drained his drink.

∼

HARRY HAD LED THE CHIEF INTO A BACK ROOM WHERE THEY watched video of Tiffany. She was only in view for a few moments, but it was long enough. As he stared at Tiffany's frozen image on the screen, the chief was certain he'd seen her before. When he remembered where, he wondered what it meant.

Greene was sure that Tiffany was the female half of the couple who had helped Melissa Bellamy pour her drunken husband back into his car on the night he was kidnapped. If so, it would be quite a coincidence if Bellamy's mistress just happened to run into him and his wife.

And who was the guy she'd been with? The chief remembered the FBI had cleared them but had yet to interview them. The people at the restaurant reported that the couple had stayed late before going up to their room. The hotel would have additional video showing the couple, as well as a record of their movements in and out of their room.

"Bellamy sure attracts the hot babes," Harry said.

"So would you if you had his money," the chief said. "I need a copy of this."

"I already sent it in an email to the department's website. You think this girl is involved in the kidnapping?"

"That's what I hope to find out," Chief Greene said.

Harry balanced himself on a beer keg and popped a

mint in his mouth. After sucking on the sweet for a moment, he reached over and grabbed a sheet of paper lying on the desk.

"There were a couple of hard cases in here earlier. They passed out these flyers with a sketch of a guy's face on them. It looks like a wanted poster. If I was the guy they're looking for, I'd be worried."

The chief studied the flyer that came from the Leffler brothers and saw that there was a phone number to call.

Tiffany had done a fair job of capturing Tanner's likeness, except for the eyes, which she had drawn tame and wearing spectacles. The reward was for a thousand dollars and gave Tanner's name as Paul Diehl, the alias he'd been using.

"Did they say why they wanted this guy?"

"No, Chief, but I'd bet real money they'll put a hurt on him when they find him."

Chief Greene stared at the flyer and wondered if there was a connection to the kidnapping.

∽

AT THE BELLAMY ESTATE, MELISSA WAS NOT HAPPY WITH the FBI. She had been counting on them to kill Tanner, or at the very least, capture him. Instead, they had made matters worse. Now Tanner would want her dead too.

She screamed at Agents Williams and Willis and cursed their incompetence before breaking down and sobbing. Everyone present, other than Fairfax and Sammy, thought that Melissa was weeping with worry for her husband.

Whatever the reason for her tears, Fairfax knew it concerned Melissa and Melissa alone. He might be obsessed with her, but Fairfax was well aware what motivated the woman—self-interest. As for Sammy,

Melissa had told him that the man who got away was the hit man out to kill Jack. Melissa was worried that Tanner might come after her.

Melissa left her home through the patio doors and sat in a lounge chair. Sammy had followed her outside and knelt down beside her.

"Why are you crying?"

"That hit man who killed Carl is still out there somewhere. He could ruin everything if he kills Jack too soon."

"Too soon? What's that mean?"

"If Jack died before midnight tomorrow it would be the same as if he divorced me. That means we would have done all this for nothing."

Sammy studied her face. "Larry and Tiffany won't kill Jack though, right?"

"No, you know the plan. Once the deadline has come and gone they'll let Jack think he escaped on his own."

"And what about the hit man?"

"The damn FBI should have killed him tonight, but that's okay. Carl's cousins are looking for him. They'll kill him."

"I don't know them. Are they as nice as Carl was?"

Melissa's laugh sounded like a choked sob. "No, Sammy. Joe and Billy Leffler are not nice."

"They won't kill Jack, will they?"

"Enough talk. Go inside before someone grows suspicious about us. And keep your mouth shut. Everything will work out and Jack will be home soon."

Sammy stood, gave Melissa a doubtful look, then drifted back into the house.

Fairfax gazed over at Sammy Bellamy as he came in and thought the boy appeared nervous. If there was a weak link in Melissa's plan, it was Sammy. Fairfax walked over to where Sammy had just slumped onto a sofa and gestured for him to get up again.

"When was the last time you ate?"

Sammy thought about it, then said, "This morning."

"Let's go into the kitchen and get ourselves some food. We could be in for a long night."

∾

A short time later, Fairfax was serving Sammy a plate of eggs over easy with hash browns, ham, and toast. His own plate contained a scrambled egg and an onion bagel.

"I didn't know you could cook, Mr. Fairfax," Sammy said.

"Only simple meals like this. I worked my way through college as a short-order cook."

They weren't alone when they entered the kitchen, as three FBI agents had been huddled in a corner discussing the fiasco in the woods. They eventually figured out Tanner had left the scene by driving a vehicle that resembled a police cruiser. The helicopter had flown over it three separate times without giving it a thought. The security guard who was responsible for guarding the property had talked to a reporter and made the agents sound like buffoons. In addition, the guard's damn dog, Denny, had mauled their dog to the point that he needed stitches.

If that wasn't bad enough, one agent had wounded another after a round had passed through one of Tanner's cardboard outlines. The man had only suffered a minor wound to his hand, but it counted as a friendly fire incident and would engender massive paperwork and an investigation. Worse of all, they were long hours into the kidnapping and no closer to bringing the victim home.

Once the agents left and Fairfax was alone with Sammy, he asked him a question.

"You're worried about your brother, aren't you?"

"Yeah."

"Why?"

"Because he's been kidnapped."

"No, it's more than that. You're afraid that Jack might get killed."

"It could happen."

Fairfax sent Sammy the sort of compassionate smile that an uncle might give him.

"Your brother cares a great deal about you, do you know that?"

"Jack? This house has eight bedrooms, and he makes me live above the garage."

"He has trouble displaying his true feelings, but you are his only family."

"Jack says if I didn't look so much like our father that he would have tossed me in the gutter."

"What Jack says and how Jack feels are two different things. He lets you live here because he loves you, and God forbid, if anything should happen to him, you'll be taken care of."

Sammy licked butter off his fingers, then said, "What do you mean?"

"As you know, I'm Jack's attorney."

"Yeah?"

"I know what's in his will, Sammy. Although I'm prohibited from giving you details, well, as I stated earlier, you are his only family."

Sammy's mouth hung open as he blinked several times. "Are you saying he's left me everything?"

Fairfax held up a hand. "I did not say that. However, you are mentioned in Jack's will."

Sammy leaned back in his seat, and Fairfax saw that his eyes had grown moist.

"I thought Jack only tolerated me."

"He's the type of man who uses bluster to disguise his true feelings."

"I guess so," Sammy said as he stood. He reached out a greasy hand toward Fairfax. Fairfax shook it and fought the urge to make a face of displeasure. "Thank you, Mr. Fairfax, for the food, and the talk."

"You're welcome, Sammy, and come to me any time you're troubled."

"I'll do that," Sammy said.

Fairfax rose from his seat after Sammy left the room and washed his hands at the kitchen sink. He hadn't lied, not really. Sammy was mentioned in Jack Bellamy's will, which was a video will. In it, Jack left Sammy exactly one penny. He only gave him that much, so Sammy couldn't claim he was excluded from the will by mistake.

Fairfax could tell that Sammy was losing his nerve. If he confessed the kidnapping was staged so that Melissa could gain millions, Melissa would be jailed, then placed out of Fairfax's reach. Far better to let the young man think that Jack's death might not be all bad. There was nothing like self-interest to stiffen the spine and ease the conscience.

17
SPEED BUMP

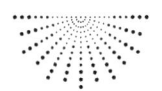

Tanner saw the man approaching fast on his left side and figured he was about to be carjacked or mugged. The guy was small, but he was holding a big gun and wearing a nylon stocking over his face. Tanner hadn't seen anyone wear a stocking for a mask in a long time.

He was stopped at a red light in what could be considered Byzantine's warehouse district. Old, red brick two-story buildings lined both sides of the street, and there was no one else around.

Tanner had dumped Hal Hanson's security guard vehicle in the parking lot of a movie theater and stolen an old, white Ford pickup. He pressed down on the clutch, slipped the gear into reverse, and shoved opened the driver's side door.

As the truck sped backwards the edge of the open door slammed into the carjacker and sent him spinning away. Tanner heard a cry of surprise followed by a grunt when the door hit the little man. Small though he was, he was tough. He rolled along the asphalt, came to rest on his stomach, then got up on his knees.

The big gun was still in his hand and he was aiming it at the windshield. Tanner had already shifted again and was giving the truck gas. The grill caught the guy in his stocking-covered face. Despite the mask he wore, the truck's headlights revealed the look of panic in his eyes. The man was laid out on his back when Tanner kept going, and for the second time that day he ran over a man who'd tried to kill him.

Tanner parked the truck and went back to look at the thug. One or more of the truck's big tires had rolled over the carjacker's right arm, which looked flattened and distorted. Death had come from his skull being slammed hard against the street.

The man probably had no connection to the kidnappers. Tanner took his wallet anyway, so he'd have his ID. When an idea came, he also took the man's keys. It was nearing midnight and Tanner had nowhere to stay. Wherever the carjacker lived, it was likely better than sleeping in the pickup truck. Although, the odds of getting any sleep at all were low. Time was running out on the contract and Bellamy had to be found.

Tanner stripped off the stocking and studied the face beneath it. He had been a white guy in his thirties and appeared unremarkable. He left the little man lying in the gutter and headed toward the address on his license. With any luck, the guy had lived alone.

~

Inside the town's police station, Chief Greene was addressing his people as a shift change was taking place. He had copies of the Leffler brothers' flyer made and was passing them out.

"This man goes by the name of Paul Diehl, but I

believe it's an alias. I also think he might have a connection to the Bellamy kidnapping."

The chief passed out more sheets of paper. This time it was a photo of Larry and Tiffany that was taken in the parking lot on the night Jack Bellamy went missing.

"These two were cleared by the FBI, but I still want to talk to them. Their names and details are at the bottom of the page. If you spot them, haul them in."

The cops were chatting among each other and grinning. Tanner was worth a grand to the Leffler brothers. Why bring him into the station when you could get cash for him on the street? To the cops in Byzantine, money trumped duty every time. Knowing this, the chief sweetened the pot on his end.

"Anyone that brings in the guy in the sketch will get two weeks off with pay. That's better than a thousand bucks."

It was, but not by much, and you had to count on the chief to keep his word. By the time roll call was over, and the cops hit the street, they were divided in their thinking. Some wanted to take the money, while others desired the time off. Tanner now had a posse in blue looking for him.

∼

Peter Fairfax hadn't been the only one concerned about Sammy holding up to the pressure. Melissa was worried about Sammy having second thoughts and cutting a deal with the FBI. While Sammy had been in the kitchen with Fairfax, Melissa had emailed Tiffany and asked her to contact the Leffler brothers for her.

A half hour later she checked the email account and saw that she had received a reply. She was to lure Sammy to the northern end of the estate, which looked down on a river. The Leffler brothers would take it from there and make it appear as if Sammy had an accident and stepped off the cliff in the dark. Why Sammy would be walking around a mile from the house Melissa didn't know, but she did know how to lure him there.

~

"Why there?" Sammy asked.

"It's private, and no one will see us," Melissa said.

They were in the laundry room and talking softly. Despite the late hour, the home was alive with activity, and FBI and police personnel were scattered throughout the house.

"Are you talking about sex?"

Melissa smiled. "I need you, Sammy. Will you meet me there?"

"Hell yeah."

"Good, but you leave first, and don't let anyone see you. Just take that dirt path past the old shed. It leads right to the cliff."

Sammy's grin was huge. "I can't wait."

Melissa watched him leave and felt relief. Soon, she'd have one less problem to deal with.

~

The little carjacker had an apartment above a corner grocery store. It was accessible by a flight of wooden stairs that were outside and attached to the side of the building.

He had lived alone, had no pets, but had a hobby. Over a hundred model cars sat on shelves. They were the kind you put together from kits. Tanner counted no less than four Batmobiles. Tanner had fond memories of building such cars with his father, but that was back when he was a kid.

The furniture was sparse but comfortable. Tanner sat in a recliner to go over his options, and that's when he saw the flyer. Someone had drawn a decent sketch of him, except for the eyes. Seeing the name of his alias listed, Tanner knew for certain that identity was burned. He had to assume the police and FBI had also seen the flyer and that he was wanted by cops and crooks alike. If it weren't for the contract, Tanner would leave Byzantine far behind. That couldn't happen, not yet; he still had a job to do.

Despite the risk, his best bet was to visit the Bellamy estate again and have another talk with Melissa. Better yet, he could abduct her and force her to lead him to her husband. That would be a difficult task, but worth it.

Tanner rose from the chair and opened the refrigerator. There were bottles of beer but no food, other than a carton of pork lo mein that had mold growing on it. There was a microwave, so he could heat something up.

After picking a deadbolt, Tanner opened a door at the rear of the apartment. It revealed an inner staircase. Moments later, he was down in the grocery store. He was looking around in the dark with the aid of a small flashlight set to low illumination.

The store carried a little bit of everything, including canned vegetables and packaged dishes that came in a box. The only other food in the store were candy bars and other snack items. Tanner was too hungry to dine on such fare and wanted real food. An odd sound drew Tanner to look behind the counter. He saw a water cooler, then heard it gurgle again. It was the kind with the five-gallon jug on top.

With his tour of the store completed, Tanner returned

to the apartment. After stashing away his spare weapons and gear, including the gun that had been owned by the carjacker, he went back out into the night. It was too risky to go to a bar that served food, but he remembered seeing a convenience store several blocks away that he could stroll to in a few minutes. They should at least have a frozen dinner he could heat up in the microwave.

Tanner walked the midnight streets of Byzantine, unaware that a pair of eyes were watching his every move.

~

THE OLD WOMAN WHO OWNED THE GROCERY STORE LIVED across the street from it in a small home she also owned. Her name was Sadie Dillingham. Sadie was eighty-two, spry, and in her earlier years had worked as a hooker.

Sadie had noticed the light come on in her tenant's apartment. When the lights went out, she saw that the man leaving the apartment was definitely not her tenant, who was a short man named Nate.

As he passed beneath a streetlight, Sadie saw the man's face. When she compared it to the flyer she'd received earlier, she thought they were a match. Sadie, a lifelong resident of Byzantine knew a good thing when it fell into her lap. She muted her TV, picked up the phone, and decided to cash in.

18
MIGHTIER THAN THE SWORD

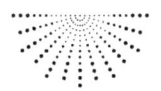

The northern edge of Jack Bellamy's estate was bordered by a river. This section of the waterway was shallow and dotted with rocks. It had been narrower for most of its existence, but that had been changing. Decades earlier, the land had joined the water at the edge of a long hill. Time had eroded the hill until it became a cliff.

The people who owned the land back in the nineties erected a wooden fence for safety purposes. That fence was gone, along with an additional acre of the land it had sat on, trees and all. During Hurricane Sandy, more of the land eroded. At the present time, the river flowed forty-three feet below the jagged edge of the cliff.

Several trees were precipitously close to the edge and leaning over. When a little more erosion took place, they too would join the water and be washed away. Then again, given the height and thickness of one of them, it might stretch across the gulf and make a natural bridge someday.

Sammy Bellamy paced near the edge as he waited for Melissa to join him. Thanks to the moonlight, he could see the path well. When the sound of footfalls came, Sammy grinned in anticipation of the pleasure he would soon be feeling. Unfortunately for Sammy, all that was headed his way was pain. The Leffler brothers charged at Sammy, with Joe on his right side and Billy on the left.

Sammy was too startled to react in time as strong hands grabbed his arms and dragged him backwards.

"Hey! Hey! Hey!" Sammy said. That was followed by a scream, after he was shoved backwards off the cliff and toward the dark water below.

When the scream ended abruptly, Joe smiled at his brother. "He should have watched where he was walking."

"Accidents will happen," Billy agreed.

"They happen more often when we're around," Joe said. The phone in his pocket vibrated and he saw that someone had left a message for him.

"Who's that, Tiffany again?" Billy asked.

"No, someone says they know where to find that hit man. They want to know if the offer is still good."

"Tell the dumbass to call back when they have him and to quit wasting our time."

"I am, but this is a good sign. It means those flyers are working."

"Let's go find a bar and down some beers; maybe the dumbass will call back soon."

"If they don't, someone else will call. That hit man will wish he never killed Carl."

~

AFTER FINDING OUT WHERE TIFFANY WAS STAYING, CHIEF Greene visited her apartment. When no one answered his knocking, he grabbed the knob and pressed his weight against the door. It took several seconds of pressure before the wooden door frame cracked and released its grip on the deadbolt with a splintering creak.

Greene entered with his gun out, but it was hanging loosely at his side. His flashlight was up, and what it showed him was revealing. The apartment was empty save for a set of four air mattresses in different corners of the living room. Judging by the bottle of window cleaner and the rags sitting in the sink, the place might have been wiped down too.

Greene knew without checking that Tiffany had leased the apartment under a phony name and that she had paid for it with money she'd stolen. The apartment had served as a headquarters of sorts for the kidnappers while they made their plans. They hadn't even bothered to have the electricity turned on.

After searching in vain for anything resembling a clue, the chief called into the station. It was time to put an APB out on Tiffany and Larry. Greene didn't know how they had managed to convince the FBI that they had an alibi for the time Bellamy went missing, but something was hinky. And for the first time, the chief wondered if Melissa Bellamy was involved in her husband's kidnapping.

∽

TANNER ENTERED THE CONVENIENCE STORE AND HEADED for the freezers at the rear. As he hoped it would, the store had a supply of frozen dinners. There were only two other customers, along with a bored-looking cashier. The store clerk was an Indian kid in his late-teens. He was watching a sitcom on a small TV and ignoring the textbook he had open on the counter.

One of the customers was a guy in his forties. He was wearing a wrinkled suit and was checking out a rack of magazines. He had on a pair of green neon headphones and heavy metal music leaked out from them. The other customer was a beautiful young woman with reddish-blonde hair, who was one aisle over. The shelving was short, only about five-feet high, and so Tanner could make her out from the neck up. If her body matched her face, she would be something else.

When Tanner caught her staring at him, she sent him a smile. It wasn't so long ago that Tanner would have attempted to hook-up with the twenty-something looker, with the added benefit of having a safe place to stay.

But that was before Sara, and so all he had to offer her back was a smile and a nod. The woman turned away and eased down the aisle. There was a security mirror positioned up high in one corner. Tanner used it to watch her, as he peeked out from under the long-billed cap he was wearing. She had removed two items from the purse hanging off her shoulder. One was a gun, the other was a badge. She was an off-duty cop. She turned around to look at Tanner again while keeping her hands below the level of the shelving. This time the smile was seductive, as she walked back to where she'd stood before.

"Hi."

Tanner smiled back at her. "I was hoping you'd start a conversation."

"Why didn't you start one?"

"I'm the shy type."

"You might be shy, but I guess you're not alone, hmm?" she said, and the voice was as sexy as her looks.

"What makes you think I don't live alone?"

"I saw you take two TV dinners out of the freezer."

"Maybe I'm a big eater."

"Or maybe you have a partner, like a kidnapping partner?"

The gun was coming into view when Tanner squirted her in the eyes with pepper spray from the pen he carried. When she opened her mouth to cry out, he shot the pen's last squirt down her throat. She tossed her badge and gun on a shelf to free her hands then rubbed frantically at her face. Along with the burning in her eyes, she was gagging on the spray, and crashed back into the shelves behind her.

Tanner walked around to pick up her gun and badge. Looking down at her, he could see that she was in distress. He reached for a quart-size bottle of spring water sitting on the shelf. After opening it, he poured most of it over her face, before pressing the bottle into her hand.

"That's water; drink it."

She was retching too hard to comply with his instructions at first, but by the time he'd reached the counter, the cop was guzzling the water down to soothe her throat.

The Indian kid was staring at Tanner with a mixture of fear and confusion. Tanner tossed a twenty his way and headed out the door.

The guy reading the magazines never even looked up.

19

HANGING AROUND

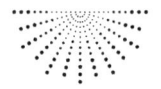

Sammy Bellamy let out a moan as he regained consciousness. When he opened his eyes, a cry of fright issued forth, as he wondered what the hell had happened to him. Sammy was hanging upside down with his back pressed against the cliff face.

His right foot had become entangled in an old and gnarled tree root that was sticking out from the cliff's surface. After overcoming the urge to panic, Sammy assessed his situation. One thing was clear. There was a good chance he was going to die.

The tree root halted his fall, after a burr on it caught hold of a shoelace. The sudden stop had caused Sammy to slam his head against the side of the cliff and strained a ligament in his ankle. It throbbed with pain as it swelled up. He had fallen over twenty feet and was still high above the water, which glistened in the moonlight.

There was no way to know if there were rocks beneath the surface, and a fall into the water could still prove fatal. A climb up might be possible, if his ankle could stand any pressure. The tree root he was tangled in wasn't the only one sticking out from the cliff. Sammy was leaning toward trying to climb up when his shoelace snapped, and his foot came free. If he hadn't turned sideways while he was falling, he would have broken his neck.

When he stood up at the edge of the river, he found his head was above water. Standing was tough due to the current and his injury, but he managed to limp onto a strip of muddy land at the base of the cliff. After gathering himself, Sammy moved along the shore, and when it widened, he was able to step on firmer ground.

His head throbbed, and the ankle hurt like hell. And yet, he could limp along on it in his loose-fitting sneaker. After finding a tree branch he could use as a crutch, things became easier.

His phone was dead, having been submerged in the water. When it struck him how close he'd come to dying, Sammy sat down and cried. Melissa had set him up. He had no idea who the two men were who'd tossed him over the cliff, but he knew that Melissa must have sent them there.

Sammy sat shivering in wet clothes as he thought over his situation. He concluded he was fucked. Melissa and the others wanted him dead, and they would kill Jack too. The FBI might keep him alive, but they would also lock him away for years.

The path that led back to the house was high above him. Sammy went in the other direction, where he might possibly find someone who could help him. After limping for over a mile along an old farm road that was all dirt and weeds, he reached his destination.

It was after one a.m., so Sammy had expected the house to be dark, but no, there were lights still on. His arrival was hardly a quiet one as he thumped his way up onto the porch with the branch acting as his cane.

The exterior lights came on, followed by the sound of a deadbolt being unlatched. When the door cracked open an inch, a face appeared. On it, was a look of surprise.

"Sammy? Why are you here?"

"I need to talk to you. I...I need advice, like lawyer advice."

"Is this about Jack?"

Sammy began crying, he couldn't help himself. He didn't like Jack much, but he didn't hate him either, and because of his stupidity, Jack was going to die. After wiping away tears, Sammy pleaded.

"I need help. Will you help me?"

The door swung wide as the man inside the home bid Sammy to enter. He was dressed in white pajamas and wore a red silk robe over them. He had been concealing a Benelli shotgun, which he set aside. The man's name was Grant Dixon. He was known to be Jack Bellamy's oldest friend. He was also the man who'd hired Tanner to kill Bellamy.

Sammy limped into the house and began telling Dixon his story.

∽

TANNER WAS BACK AT THE APARTMENT OVER THE LITTLE corner store. He was heating up one of the dinners he'd bought by using the microwave, when he heard footsteps coming up the stairs.

It was an old woman who Tanner guessed was twice his age, given her wizened features. Despite her years, she came up the steps at a quick clip. When she smiled, Tanner saw that good dental hygiene hadn't been a priority for the woman. The few teeth that weren't missing were as yellow as corn kernels, while her breath was far from fresh.

"My name is Sadie; I'm the landlady."

Tanner recalled the name he'd read on the carjacker's driver's license.

"I'm Nate's cousin, Paul."

Sadie stuck her head in the door and looked around. "Where's Nate?"

"He was hit by a car."

"Damn! How bad off is he?"

"He hurt his arm."

"Too bad, but you can't stay here, mister. Nate owes me back rent."

"How much is it?"

"Four hundred dollars."

"I can take care of that for Nate," Tanner said. He took out his wallet and reached in to remove cash. Sadie licked her lips in anticipation and snatched the money from his hand as he was handing it to her.

After cackling, she turned from the door and headed down the stairs.

"It was nice doing business with you."

Tanner watched her go and reminded himself to keep the dental appointment he had scheduled for later in the month.

～

THE OLD LADY HAD BEEN GONE FOR ONLY A MINUTE WHEN Tanner heard more footsteps. They weren't the quick steps that Sadie had made on the outer stairway. They were furtive steps, and they were coming from the staircase that led down into the little store.

Tanner took out his gun and checked the window. Down below was a police car, and coming up the stairs was a cop. A voice called out from beyond the locked door leading to the shop below.

"Paul Diehl. This is the police. My partner and I have you surrounded. Step outside with your hands in the air and you won't be hurt."

Tanner grimaced as he wondered if he had been followed from the store. He was certain he hadn't been and wondered how they had located him. In any event, he would give himself up. Killing cops, even the crooked cops of the Byzantine police force, was not something he would do. Besides, there were only two of them. Far better to deal with a pair of cops than to wait for a SWAT team to show up.

Tanner announced his intention to cooperate and stepped outside with his hands up. As a blond cop approached him on the exterior staircase, the other cop, a dark-haired man, used a key to open the door inside the apartment. They cuffed his hands behind his back and pocketed the weapon he'd sat on the scarred kitchen table. Before they could lead him downstairs, Sadie appeared through the doorway the dark-haired cop had used.

"Hey, mister?"

"Yeah?" Tanner said.

"I'm the one that turned you in. How do you like that?"

"I don't."

"Here's something else you won't like. Nate didn't owe me any rent."

Sadie cackled like the old crow she was, as Tanner was led down the stairs.

20

NO HONOR AMONG THIEVES

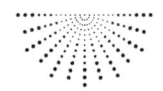

Sammy had changed out of his wet clothes and was sitting on Dixon's sofa wearing one of the lawyer's robes. It was made of silk like the red robe Dixon wore, but Sammy's was black. The garment was loose on Dixon, but tight on the muscular Sammy. As he told Dixon his story, he held an ice pack to his swollen ankle.

Dixon had handed Sammy a bottle of beer, while he sipped on Scotch. The boy's story fascinated Dixon, while giving him hope that Jack Bellamy might die yet. He sat across from Sammy in a leather wing chair.

"How long ago was it that Melissa first mentioned the kidnapping to you?" Dixon asked.

"About a month."

"And were you already lovers?"

"That started months ago."

"She still used sex to make you betray your brother. And how old were you at the time?"

"Nineteen, I've been nineteen for a few months now."

"Too bad you weren't still a minor when the affair

started. That might have helped you… that is, if this ever gets before a jury."

"Mr. Dixon, I don't want to go to prison."

"I'll do what I can for you, Sammy, you know that, but I'm afraid this is quite a mess."

"She tried to have me killed. It still blows my mind that Melissa wants me dead."

"You've outlived your usefulness. And let me guess, you were having second thoughts?"

"Not really, I just didn't want anyone to kill Jack. And oh yeah, there's also a hit man out to get him."

At Sammy's mention of Tanner, Dixon choked a little on his Scotch.

"What's this about a hit man?"

"He tried to kill Jack, but he killed a friend of Melissa's instead."

"Was it an accident?"

Sammy went on to explain about Carl masquerading as Bellamy, and the consequences that befell him. That answered a few things for Dixon. Such as how Jack Bellamy had survived Tanner. The bastard's luck was unbelievable.

"Anyway, the guy is still around. If Melissa doesn't kill Jack, this hit man will."

Dixon got up from his chair and went to the wet bar in the corner of his living room. When he returned, he handed Sammy another beer, then settled down with the fresh drink he'd poured himself. He had downed four drinks before Sammy had shown up. A love of liquor was something that Dixon and Jack Bellamy had in common.

"Sammy, would you like to hire me to represent you?"

"Yes. Will you do it?"

"For now, I'll act as a legal advisor. To make it legit, give me a dollar."

Sammy fished a bill out of his wallet and passed it over to Dixon. The dollar bill was wet and felt slimy.

Dixon laid it on a table and wiped his fingers on his robe.

"Would you like my advice?"

"Hell yeah."

Dixon smiled as he said, "Do nothing."

"What's that mean?"

"Exactly as I said, do nothing. Whoever tossed you off that cliff must have told Melissa you were dead. Let them keep thinking that. If they believe you're dead, they won't come after you again."

Even Sammy saw the logic in that statement, but he had a question.

"What about Jack?"

"According to what you told me, Melissa needs Jack alive until midnight or she won't get the money promised to her. That gives the FBI almost another full day to find him and free him. The FBI rarely fails."

"You wouldn't say that if you had been out in the woods earlier. They had the hit man surrounded and he got away."

"He must be very good at what he does," Dixon said. In fact, he was counting on it.

~

THE TWO COPS STOPPED HALFWAY DOWN THE EXTERIOR staircase to argue about what to do with Tanner. The blond cop wanted to call the number on the flyer, while his dark-haired partner wanted to arrest Tanner and claim the promised two weeks off with pay.

Sadie, who was standing at the top of the staircase

interrupted them. "You boys remember now. I don't have to give you anything for six months for doing this."

"That's not up to us," said the blond cop.

"The hell you say. We had a deal. I tell you where to find this guy and I don't have to pay protection money for six months."

"It's not protection money. They're donations to the police benevolent association. If you want us to stay benevolent, you'd better keep donating."

"Damn it. We had a deal."

The dark-haired cop laughed. "File a complaint, granny."

The old woman stomped her foot. "You sons of bitches. I could have gotten a thousand dollars for him. You owe me something."

"You have our thanks, but we'll be claiming that money," the blond cop said.

"I want the two weeks off," said his partner.

The blond cop was about to respond when Tanner leapt up and kicked him in the face. The guy was standing backwards on the stairs and went tumbling down the remaining eight steps.

Tanner had landed on his side, and his left shoulder went numb as it hit the edge of a stair. The cop behind and above him on the steps took out his baton.

His first swing missed as Tanner dodged it while getting to his feet, then Tanner caught the second swing on his chest. Tanner's hands were still cuffed behind him, but his feet were free. He sent a high kick at the cop's chin. The baton dropped, the cop wobbled, and Tanner moved behind him and sent a booted foot at his ass.

The first cop had made it to his knees and was bringing out a gun when his partner landed on top of him. Tanner reached them and administered more kicks. With both cops senseless and on the verge of passing out, Tanner claimed a handcuff key and freed himself.

At the top of the steps, Sadie swore at the turn of events. When Tanner glared up at her with a gun in his hand, the old woman turned white. While making a sound of fear, Sadie rushed into the apartment and slammed the door shut.

Tanner cuffed the cops together, then secured the blond cop's other wrist to the base of a street sign with a second pair of restraints. Lights were coming on in windows across the way as the sounds of the struggle woke tenants in a small apartment building.

The blond cop, his face bloody, was still woozy, but his partner had regained his senses. He pleaded with Tanner not to shoot him. Tanner ignored him as he patted him down. He found a hidden handcuff key in a side change pocket, along with a cheap throwaway gun in an ankle holster. Once he was satisfied they would need help to get free, Tanner headed toward their patrol car.

He had also taken their service pistols, badges, and shoulder mics. Counting the off-duty female cop, he now had three police firearms. If this kept up, Tanner would single-handedly disarm the Byzantine police force. When he drove off in the patrol car, he had the lights and siren going. It was time to visit Melissa Bellamy again.

21
NO HONOR AMONG KIDNAPPERS

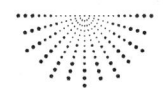

Tiffany and Larry received an email from Joe Leffler telling them that the police were looking for them. That wasn't supposed to happen. It was just one more instance of things going wrong and Larry was growing nervous.

Hell, Carl had been killed less than an hour into the kidnapping. Now Rudy was dead, and Melissa had the Leffler brothers murder Sammy ahead of schedule. Larry thought that last act was stupid. Didn't Melissa think the FBI would notice the kid went missing?

Larry yawned. He was on the first watch to keep an eye on Bellamy, while Tiffany caught a few hours of sleep after finally crashing from a coke high. Larry was beat, but Jack Bellamy looked as if he had just awakened after a full night's sleep. He was watching a program on TV that discussed foreign stock markets.

Larry didn't understand any of it and had a hard enough time figuring out his checkbook. At one point, Bellamy laughed, as on TV they were discussing a huge drop in the South Korean stock market.

"What's so funny?"

"I just made a little over two million dollars."

"How's that?"

"I shorted a foreign index fund and it dropped like a rock on Friday."

"You can make money when stocks go down?"

"If you know what you're doing you can."

"Shit, and you really made two million?"

"That's right. Now you see why I don't care about the gold I buried? And it can all be yours."

Larry looked at the closed bedroom door, then leaned forward and lowered his voice.

"I've been thinking about that. The problem is, what do I do with Tiffany?"

"Kill the bitch."

Larry winced. "I don't want to do that."

"Okay, so lock her up with me. You can hide the two of us somewhere while you go dig up the gold. Once you have it, call the cops and tell them where we are."

"That's no good either, because then Tiffany will go to prison."

"Yeah, and if she's in prison she can't go looking for you to get revenge."

Larry considered that, then nodded. "That might work."

"There's only one problem. How are you going to lock her up?"

"I'll take her by surprise and hold a gun on her."

"I told her about the gold."

"You did?"

"That's right."

Larry glared at Bellamy as if he had betrayed him. "Why did you do that?"

"I was looking to make a deal, and you didn't seem interested."

"Was she interested?"

"Tiffany was looking up gold prices. I'll bet you she's already planning where to run off to once she gets her hands on it."

Larry gazed at the bedroom door again. This time his eyes were like slits. "That devious bitch. Do you think she wants to kill me?"

"Maybe she'll just tie you up, although a bullet would be easier."

"I still don't want to kill her."

"Okay then, what's your plan? And remember, she'll be looking for you to try something."

"You could distract her for me."

"How?"

"Just be yourself and call her a name. When she turns your way, I'll pull a gun on her."

"What if she doesn't take her eyes off you?"

"Do you have a better plan?"

"Sure, unlock me from these chains so I can surprise her. When she's dealing with me, then you can hit her from behind."

"You'll try to escape."

"If I did you would shoot me."

"I sure as hell would, Bellamy, remember that. But just how are you going to surprise Tiffany? She might shoot you too."

"I'll go for the gun she keeps on her hip. While we're struggling over that, you can hit her with your own gun."

Larry made a face as he considered the plan. "I don't like the idea of releasing you from those chains."

"If I don't have enough mobility the plan might not work. You guys made the chain so short with these damn padlocks that I can barely move."

"All right, here's what I'll do. I'll unlock two of the padlocks, so you have more slack, but that's it."

"What if it's not enough?"

"It will have to be, and this is how we'll do it. I'll act like I'm asleep when Tiffany comes to relieve me. She'll be so pissed at me that she won't pay you any attention. Then, when she leans over to shake me awake, you stand up and distract her, and that's when I'll pull my gun."

"The plan would work better if you freed me all the way."

"Not gonna happen. And I'll tell you right now, if you're lying about the gold you'll wish you were never born."

"The gold is real."

"It damn well better be."

"Think of it, Larry. In a few days you'll be a rich man."

"And it's worth millions, right? You said it was worth millions."

"Absolutely, my friend. Gold, Larry, millions in gold."

22
OFFICER TANNER

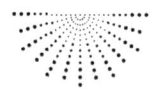

The patrol car Tanner had stolen had a few helpful accessories stored in its trunk. Along with a medical kit and a box of latex gloves, there was also a tactical vest, a set of handcuffs, and an old worn duty belt. Best of all, there was a spare uniform.

Tanner changed into the uniform, which fit loosely and had pants an inch too short. He had driven the patrol car within a thousand feet of the Bellamy estate and left it parked out on the road. It was only a matter of time before the cops used satellite tracking to find the squad car, so there was no sense in trying to hide it.

A pair of federal agents were on the front gate leading to the home, and there were two news vans still parked nearby. Tanner avoided them by climbing over a wall and walking across the lawn.

Two FBI agents were standing outside a rear door of the house and were smoking. Tanner walked right up to them while smiling. He was wearing the eyeglasses again.

"You guys make me wish I had never kicked the habit. This would be a good night to have a smoke."

"You're better off without it," said one of the agents, as Tanner opened the door to walk in.

Another agent was in the kitchen. She was a female with shoulder-length dark hair. The woman was sipping on a cup of tea and staring down at her phone. She glanced up long enough to register the blue uniform then went back to looking at her screen.

Tanner left the kitchen and eased his way up the rear staircase. Voices came from the front of the house, and for a moment, Tanner caught a glimpse of two more FBI agents. They were Agents Williams and Willis, the male and female team that were leading the investigation into the kidnapping.

Tanner stared at them longer than he should have, while wondering if they were twins.

He continued up the stairs, went around a corner, and found an empty hallway. When he came upon Melissa's bedroom door, he saw that it was closed, but there was light leaking out from under the doorway. Tanner had not expected that. It was almost two a.m. and he had been counting on Melissa being asleep. He wondered why she was still awake, and if she was alone. When he heard the murmur of two voices, a man and a woman. Tanner moved toward the door to listen.

∼

INSIDE THE ROOM, CHIEF GREENE WAS CONFRONTING Melissa about his suspicion that she was behind the kidnapping. She was wearing a robe while the chief was dressed, and both of them were standing near her bed.

Greene had been informed by phone about the patrol car being stolen, along with the sighting of Tanner at the convenience store. Given that Tanner's description roughly matched that of the man seen at the ransom drop, and that the same man was now being sought by someone, Greene was working under the assumption the kidnappers had suffered a falling out among their ranks.

The dead man found near Tanner's abandoned rental had been identified as Rudy Farrell, a known grifter. Chief Greene was certain that Jack Bellamy was never meant to survive his kidnapping. He was more determined than ever to find Bellamy and keep him safe.

"How dare you say that? I love my husband."

The chief smirked. "You mean you love his money, and I don't blame you, but nobody loves Jack Bellamy."

"Chief Greene, I resent your accusation and I want you to leave the room right now."

"Mrs. Bellamy, can I call you Melissa?"

"No."

"Whatever, but hear me out. If you think by killing Jack you'll inherit his fortune, forget it. I'll see you go to prison even if I have to frame you myself."

"I'm not involved in the kidnapping. Why don't you believe me?"

"Listen to me. I don't care if you get your hands on the ransom money. I just want Jack to be alive when all this is over."

"I thought you hated Jack, Chief. I know he has something on you."

Greene stiffened in reaction to those words, then forced a smile. "That's not true."

"Isn't it? Jack drives drunk all the time and he doesn't even get a slap on the wrist. Explain that."

"He's...um, he's a prominent citizen. That's why I cut him some slack."

"He told me about you."

"What did he say?" Greene asked, from a mouth that had gone dry.

"Once, when he was really drunk, he said he owned you."

"What did he mean by that, did he say?"

Melissa smiled. "What do you think?"

Greene bent over and grunted, as if someone had punched him in the gut.

Melissa knew nothing about Greene's secret. She was only trying to distract him from his line of questioning. Just the thought that another person knew his secret unbalanced the man. The chief reached out and gripped Melissa by her arms.

"What did Jack tell you?"

"Let go of me."

"What did he say?"

"He didn't say anything. Ow! You're hurting me."

Greene released her and took a step back. He damned himself and stared down at the floor, knowing he had come close to losing it and harming the woman.

Melissa rushed past him, flung the door open, and saw Tanner staring at her. Her scream was loud and piercing. Before turning away from her, Tanner had caught sight of Chief Greene in a mirror, although the chief couldn't see him from where he was standing. Tanner sprinted down the hallway as a house full of cops and Feds rushed up the stairs.

~

SAMMY TOLD GRANT DIXON HE'D BE FINE SLEEPING ON HIS sofa and not to bother making up a guest bedroom. After Dixon went off to get some sleep, Sammy lay in the living room and stared up at the ceiling. Jack was going to die.

His brother was going to die, and he had helped the people who were planning to do it.

Dixon's advice to lay low and do nothing seemed to be the smart move. Still, if Jack was killed and he had done nothing to stop it...

Sammy wasn't sure he could live with himself if that happened. When he spotted an odd shape hidden among the shadows near the doorway, Sammy turned on a light to get a better look at it. It turned out to be the loaded shotgun Dixon had leaned against the wall in a corner. His curiosity appeased, Sammy turned out the light and tried to sleep. His eyes kept popping open as a plan formed in his mind.

What if I rescued Jack?

Sammy lay there in the dark, as foolish thoughts flittered about his young mind.

∾

Tanner returned to the rear staircase, went down three steps, turned, and fell onto the stairs. The female Fed he'd seen in the kitchen appeared first, with the two smokers close on her heels. Tanner pulled himself up to his hands and knees and shook his head, as the woman came beside him.

"What happened?" she said.

"I got punched in the face by a male Caucasian, armed, about six-feet tall. He was after the Bellamy woman. I think he headed for the main staircase."

The three Feds moved past Tanner as they eased along the hallway with their guns drawn. Tanner had bought himself some time, but he still had to get off the property and the place was filled with cops and FBI agents.

He went out the way he'd come in and saw a pair of lit

cigarettes glowing at the foot of the steps. The two smokers must have flicked them away when they heard the scream. Tanner halted for a moment and judged the wisdom of going back inside and taking another shot at getting to Melissa. He deemed it not worth the risk and kept moving toward the wall where he'd left the patrol car.

He was certain Melissa could tell him where Bellamy was being kept, and she was the only one with that knowledge who was within reach. Then, Tanner realized there was another possibility. Whoever was handing those flyers out was either a kidnapper or someone affiliated with them. Either way, they could lead him to Bellamy. Thanks to the phone number written on the flyer, he knew how to get in touch with them.

Tanner decided he would make that call, but first, he had to get off the estate. As he neared the wall to climb over, he saw flashing lights. It seemed they had located the stolen police car. He could still climb over the wall at a different section and be gone before they began an organized search. However, that would leave him on foot.

Tanner turned around and headed back toward the house, as a better plan formed in his mind.

23
FIRE!

When Melissa spoke only of Tanner being in the house and made no mention of the chief's accusations, Greene was more certain than ever that she was guilty. An innocent woman would have been indignant and demanded the chief be barred from the investigation. And yet, if Melissa brought up the chief's allegations, others might wonder about her too.

It infuriated Greene to know that Melissa could tell him where to find Bellamy but wouldn't admit it. When things settled down, he planned to make a run at her again. For now, the chief was out cruising the area around the estate and looking for a man who was a likely accomplice of Melissa's. He was in a wooded area and aiming a spotlight toward the trees lining the road.

Whoever the intruder was, he had taken an awful risk invading the home that way. He had also beat down three cops and stolen a patrol car.

Say what you will about the guy, Greene thought. *The bastard's got balls.*

That impression was deepened in the chief's mind as a voice spoke from the rear seat.

"This is far enough. Pull over."

Greene let out a gasp of fright as he swerved his cruiser across the solid line before coming to a hard stop. Looking up into his rearview mirror he saw a set of intense eyes. They were staring back at him from behind the Plexi-glass screen that separated the two compartments. Greene was also gazing into the barrel of his own shotgun. The chief had thought he was alone, and he felt his heart doing triple-time in his chest.

"Fuck, man. You scared the shit out of me. You do realize that those doors don't open once you shut them, right? You've trapped yourself back there, asshole."

"Not while I'm holding this 12-gauge key. Now do as I say and pull this thing to the curb. I don't want you attracting attention by blocking the road."

The chief moved the vehicle against the curb and parked, while leaving the engine running. When he made a move toward his gun Tanner tapped the shotgun against the divider.

"Don't be stupid. You'd never get off a shot."

"I'm the Chief of Police. Do you know how much trouble you're in?"

"I'm not the one with a shotgun pointed at my head. Now unlock these doors, or would you rather I shoot the window glass and climb out?"

Chief Greene stepped out of his SUV with his hands in plain sight. After opening the rear door, he took three steps back to give Tanner room to exit. When Tanner was out of the vehicle, he instructed Greene to toss his gun and phone onto the front seat. With the chief unarmed, Tanner lowered the shotgun.

"I heard some of the conversation you were having with Bellamy's wife. You know she's involved."

"You're admitting she's one of your partners?"

"I'm not a kidnapper. I came to this sorry town on other business and got on their radar because of a mix-up."

"What sort of mix-up?"

"That doesn't matter, Chief. Just know that I want to find Bellamy more than you do."

"Why?"

"Someone's paying me to do so."

"There's a reward out for you, did you know that?"

"Your cops already tried cashing me in. Who's offering the money?"

"I heard a rumor it was two independent contractors from out of town."

"Hit men?"

"More like goons for hire."

Tanner raised the shotgun and told the chief to start walking.

"What's your name?" the chief said. "And don't tell me it's Paul Diehl. I know that's an alias."

"You don't need my name, and I'll be gone soon."

"You'll be locked up is what you'll be, mister, or dead. Hand me that shotgun and I'll make sure no one can get to you."

"You should start walking, Chief; it's a long way back to the house."

Tanner climbed into the vehicle and drove away. When he looked in the rearview mirror, he saw that the chief was giving him the finger. Classy, Byzantine was definitely a classy town.

∼

Back at the Bellamy estate, Melissa was in the living room and addressing those present.

"I'll pay ten-thousand dollars to anyone who finds the man who broke in here tonight, and I don't care if he's dead or alive."

The statement made the Byzantine cops smile, while getting groans from the FBI. When it was pointed out to Melissa she would be better served offering a reward for the kidnappers, she laughed.

"The man that came here tonight is one of the kidnappers. He's probably their leader, and you let him get away—again."

"He may yet be apprehended, ma'am," said Agent Willis.

"Good, and I hope he's killed in a shootout."

"It would be better if he were captured, ma'am. That way he could lead us to your husband."

"Oh, yes, that would be better," Melissa said. When she looked over at Peter Fairfax, she saw that the old lawyer was wearing that damn smile again.

~

Tanner came across a drunk who had crashed his car into a mailbox. The vehicle was an old green Chevy Cavalier. When the man saw Tanner walking toward him in the police uniform. He lowered his window and said, "Evening, Ociffer, I mean, Officer."

"How much have you had to drink this evening, sir?"

"I'm not drunk."

"License and registration, please."

"I don't have them; some bastard picked my pocket earlier."

"There's a lot of that going around I hear."

"I had eighty bucks in that wallet."

"What's your name?"

"Joe Spinner."

"Where do you live, Mr. Spinner?"

"I'm just a few blocks from here, you know, by the bakery."

"Mr. Spinner, you have a choice. Take a breathalyzer test and risk losing your license, or you can let me impound your vehicle and start walking home."

Spinner hiccupped before asking a question. "Will I ever get my car back?"

"Show up at the station tomorrow evening after six and your vehicle will be returned."

Spinner thought that over with his pickled brain and found that it made perfect sense.

"It's a deal. I hate blowing into that damn machine."

"And I would hate to arrest you. Have a good night, sir."

Spinner weaved his way to the nearest corner and went right. Seconds later, Tanner was driving off in his car.

∾

Tanner's next stop was a return to the corner grocery store where he had escaped from the cops. Their fellow officers had freed them, and the building looked dark and silent. Tanner drove past it, parked half a block away, then traveled back on foot.

He had left his spare weapons hidden inside the apartment along with other things he might need. Retrieving them was worth the risk of running into the old lady again. Besides, maybe she had learned to mind her own business. She'd looked terrified when he'd last seen her.

Tanner had just taken a vent cover off to claim his things when he heard the sound of car doors opening and closing. He grabbed his items from their hiding place and looked outside. There were two men dressed in dark hoodies out there standing beside a black Cadillac Escalade. The two were tall, broad, and carrying handguns. The tallest of the pair had something else in his other hand. It looked metallic, but Tanner was too far away to make out details at night.

A hammering sound came from across the room. Tanner spun with his gun up and ready in a two-handed grip, then saw an odd sight. It was the tip of a long nail. As the hammering continued, more nails were driven into the door. When the cackling laugh came, Tanner knew it was Sadie doing the hammering.

"You're trapped now, mister, and those two boys downstairs aren't as stupid as the cops you got away from earlier."

Tanner went back to the window and saw that the men had split up. One of them must have moved to the rear door downstairs at the back of the shop.

"You're worth a thousand dollars to those two," Sadie said through the door.

"Who are they?" Tanner asked. He was opening drawers in the kitchen as he searched for something he'd remember spotting earlier.

"They called each other Joe and Billy. When they heard you had been here, they came by to see me and ask about you. I told them what had happened, and then they left. One minute later, I see you walking back up the stairs outside. Looks like I'm getting paid for you anyway."

"Hey, Sadie?"

"What?"

"Did you ever consider that those men won't want a witness to see what they plan to do to me?"

"What's that mean?"

"Those men want to kill me, and they'll probably kill you too."

"You can't scare me."

"I'm not trying to; I'm just telling you the truth."

Tanner had found what he'd been looking for, a slot-head screwdriver and a hammer that the carjacker Nate kept in a kitchen drawer. He pressed the tip of the screwdriver against the lip of a hinge pin then struck the screwdriver with the hammer.

The pin flew out and the top hinge on the door separated. Two more hard whacks took care of the other two pins. Tanner then opened the door by pulling on the hinge side instead of at the doorknob area that had all the nails driven into it. The wooden door creaked as Tanner squeezed through the opening and Sadie let out a shriek.

Tanner raised a hand in a calming motion. "I won't hurt you, but I was serious about those men. They will kill you."

Sadie was moving down the steps with surprising speed for an old lady. However, after reaching the bottom step, she quit running and stared toward the shop door.

"Oh, Lordy no!"

Tanner had come down to stand beside her. When he followed her gaze, he saw the flickering orange glow. Glancing toward the door at the rear, more light danced at the crack beneath it. A window broke upstairs as something was thrown through the glass, that was followed by a *whooshing* sound, and more light began dancing at the top of the stairs. Tanner realized what the metal object he'd seen in one of the men's hands had been. It was a can of lighter fluid.

The Leffler brothers had found Tanner, and they were planning to roast him alive.

24

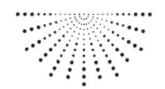

TRAPPED!

Tanner shook Sadie's shoulder to get her attention. When she turned to look at him, he could tell she had forgotten he was there.

"We're gonna die," she whined.

"No, we're not. We'll get out of here. Do you have a fire extinguisher?"

The old face transformed from terrified to hopeful in a flash. "I got one! It's behind the counter."

Tanner followed her to the sales counter and watched as she reached beneath it. When her hand reappeared, it was dragging a dusty red fire extinguisher along a shelf. Tanner took it from her and frowned as he felt the weight. It was a large cylinder, but it felt light.

Tanner was still wearing the police duty belt, which held a flashlight. When he used the light to read the date etched onto the fire extinguisher he knew that it was worthless.

"This thing is over twenty years old."

"Is that bad?"

Tanner answered her by pulling free the pin and

aiming the nozzle at the floor. The cylinder wheezed and released no fluid. As Sadie hung her head and cried, Tanner's mind raced for a way to survive.

∽

OUTSIDE THE SHOP, BILLY JOINED JOE BACK AT THE FRONT of the building.

"What are you doing here? You need to watch the back door."

"After I started the fire I pushed a dumpster in front of the door. Ain't nobody getting out that way."

"When we're sure this prick is dead we'll go put a bullet in the old woman across the street."

"Why?" Billy asked, and Joe gave him one of those looks that told him he was being thick-headed again.

"Think about it. She's seen us up close and can identify us, plus, we're burning down her business."

"Oh yeah, and we don't have to pay her the thousand dollars either."

"It won't do her any good if she's dead," Joe said.

Lights came on in several windows at the apartment house opposite the side of the building. When a window on the third floor went up and a face peeked out, Joe fired a shot that hit the brick wall a foot from the opening. The face disappeared, and all the lights that had just come on went out.

"Nosey bastards," Billy said.

∽

TANNER GAVE SADIE A SHAKE TO GET HER ATTENTION AND the old woman looked up at him with wet eyes.

"We can still get out of here if we act fast. I need you

to get me two bottles of vinegar, a box of baking soda, and dish detergent."

"What good is that stuff?"

Tanner turned around and grabbed the jug off the water cooler.

"We're going to make our own fire extinguisher."

"Huh?"

"Just gather those items, vinegar, baking soda, and detergent."

Sadie repeated the short list, then moved toward the shelves. Tanner followed with the five-gallon jug of spring water, which was about three-quarters full.

He was near the front door of the shop which was engulfed in flames and giving off black smoke. Thankfully, with the apartment door open at the top of the inner staircase, the air current was sweeping the smoke upwards. Within minutes, smoke would fill the store and make it impossible to take a clean breath. Along with that was the heat, which was already stifling and causing Tanner to sweat profusely.

Sadie brought him the vinegar first. Tanner began pouring it in through the opening at the top of the water jug. As she went back to get the other items Tanner added one to the list.

"I'll need toilet paper too!" he called loudly, so as to be heard over the crackling sounds of the flames.

Sadie had been standing near a display of toilet tissue and tossed one over to Tanner. He opened the package, unfurled some of the thin paper and began fashioning it into a cone-shaped tube. By the time Sadie returned with the other items, she had to bend over to avoid the smoke.

"That doesn't look like enough water to put out the blaze eating that door," Sadie said.

"We won't be relying on the water alone. We'll be using

a chemical reaction to douse the flames. It should give us enough time to get out. But let me go first, I'm sure they'll be shooting at us."

After adding several squirts of the dishwashing liquid into the mix inside the bottle, Tanner opened up the box of baking soda, which was nothing more than sodium bicarbonate.

When sodium bicarbonate is mixed with vinegar it causes a reaction that produces CO_2 or carbon dioxide. The result is a bubbling, foamy liquid that will smother flames, much like a fire extinguisher.

After pouring baking soda into the cone he'd fashioned from the toilet paper, Tanner used it to plug the opening of the 5-gallon jug. It was tougher than it should have been because smoke was making his eyes water and tickling his throat.

"Here we go," Tanner said. He clamped one hand over the opening of the bottle as he lifted it and gave it several hard shakes. Although he couldn't see the reaction taking place due to the smoke, he felt the pressure building in the bottle and removed his hand.

White foam shot out in a geyser and splattered the flames eating at the debris between the door frame. Most of the shop door itself was gone, having been burned away. The bottle ran out of foam far sooner than Tanner would have liked, but it had been enough to create a temporary gap between the flames.

Tanner felt himself being jostled aside as Sadie pushed past him.

"Let me out!"

"No! Wait!" Tanner said in warning, but it was too late. Gunfire erupted, and Sadie let out a scream.

A VICTIM OF CIRCUMSTANCE

The Leffler brothers had been certain the fire had taken care of their problem, while being unaware that Sadie was inside the store as well. When Tanner's homemade fire extinguisher smothered the flames blocking the front entrance, they took out their guns and aimed them at the doorway.

They hadn't realized they were shooting at Sadie until they had each placed three rounds into her. As they were looking down at the body, Tanner erupted from the building with Chief Greene's shotgun leading the way.

Joe Leffler caught a 12-gauge blast to the chest that stopped his heart by obliterating it. His body spun and slammed against his brother. The impact knocked Billy to the ground, with Joe landing on top of him. Billy felt his brother's blood drip into his eyes, and it blinded him. He wiped at his face in a panic with one hand while firing left to right in the hope of hitting Tanner.

By the time Billy could see again sirens were approaching, and Tanner was gone.

"Maybe I wounded the bastard and he ran off, Joe." When there was no answer, Billy looked down and saw that his brother was dead, and not merely wounded as he had hoped.

What was left of the staircase on the side of the building crashed into the street. It threw up sparks and spread ash, as flames destroyed the store and the apartment above it.

Billy walked past Sadie's corpse and headed toward his car. For the first time since he was a child, he cried.

∽

Tanner was slumped down behind the wheel of the vehicle he had acquired from the drunk and watched Billy drive away. When Tanner looked down at the phone in his hand, he was pleased to see that the magnetic tracking device he'd slapped on the Escalade was working.

He could have ended Billy as easily as he'd killed his brother, but the thug was more valuable to him alive. Tanner was counting on Billy leading him to the kidnappers, and to his target, Jack Bellamy. Tanner pulled away from the curb as the fire engine came into view, and he followed Billy Leffler into the deepening night.

25

TABLES TURNED

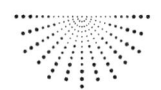

Larry heard the alarm clock in the master bedroom sound off. That meant Tiffany would be coming out soon to join them. She was supposed to take over watching Bellamy at six a.m., which was only fifteen minutes away. It was still dark outside, but the birds had begun to sing as dawn approached.

Bellamy and Larry went over their plan again before Larry removed two of the padlocks from the chain attached to Bellamy's ankle.

The extended length made it possible for Bellamy to get close to the sofa, where Larry was feigning being asleep. To make it easier to grab, Larry slid his gun just out of sight beneath the sofa, while resting his hand on the floor.

When Tiffany stepped out of the bedroom minutes later, both Larry and Bellamy pretended to be snoozing. Bellamy heard Tiffany move toward Larry. He cracked open an eye, as he prepared to distract her. His plans changed when Tiffany brought up the gun she'd been holding and shot Larry twice in the back of the head.

Bellamy bolted upright in the recliner, causing the chains to rattle like bones. "Holy shit!"

When Tiffany turned her head to look at him, he saw both sorrow and anger in her eyes. There was also a trace of white powder beneath her nose.

"You better not have been lying about that gold, Jack. Not after what I just did."

Bellamy had to swallow hard before he could answer her. "It's the truth, I swear it is."

Tiffany nodded, then headed toward the kitchen. "I need coffee."

Bellamy stared over at Larry's body and felt a shiver go down his spine. *What a cold bitch.*

Tiffany had lured him into being kidnapped by using her body. Now, she was selling out her so-called friends, while murdering one of them. Bellamy was no saint, far from it, but even he found her actions abhorrent. He looked toward the kitchen where Tiffany puttered about. If he got the chance, he'd make her suffer.

~

TANNER HAD FOLLOWED BILLY LEFFLER TO AN OLD MOTEL and watched him enter a room. Not for a moment did Tanner believe Jack Bellamy was being held there, as the place was too public. Billy was regrouping and cleaning up. He was covered in blood and had just lost his partner, whom Tanner suspected had been a brother, given their strong resemblance to each other.

After a police car entered the parking lot and began cruising slowly along, Tanner decided to leave via the other exit. He could follow Leffler's movements by use of the tracker he'd placed on his vehicle. Besides, with half the town looking for him, it was better to lie low.

To accomplish that, Tanner went back to the place where it all began, Jack Bellamy's love nest. The door lock was easy to pick, and no one had armed the alarm system.

The only clothing Tanner had was the police uniform he wore. It smelled of smoke and was sour with sweat. Bellamy kept a robe in the closet. Tanner changed into it and went looking for a washing machine. He found a washer/dryer combo in the home's basement and shoved the police uniform inside it. When he spotted the large chest freezer, he remembered he still hadn't eaten, since the police had interrupted his meal at the carjacker's apartment. After opening the freezer and looking inside, all thoughts of food left his mind. Tanner had just discovered where Rudy had hidden Carl Leffler's body.

~

Tiffany tried to move Larry's corpse and realized he was too heavy for her. After getting the idea to push the body onto a tarp, so that she could drag it, she went outside. There was a small shed in the back of the property, along with an open grave.

Carl, Larry, and Rudy had dug the deep hole for Bellamy the day before the kidnapping. Now all three men were dead, and it looked like Larry would take Bellamy's place in the dank pit.

As she opened the door to go outside, Tiffany turned and spoke to Bellamy. "I'll be back in less than a minute. Don't try anything."

Bellamy shrugged. "Why would I? You'll soon have the gold and I'll have my freedom."

"Remember that," she said, as she left.

Bellamy waited ten seconds. He assumed that should be enough time for Tiffany to get far away from the house, so she wouldn't hear the chains rattling. When he was ready to move, he got down on the floor and crawled on his hands and knees toward the sofa. He had just enough slack in the chain to reach the gun Larry had hidden beneath it. When the side of his hand touched Larry's cooling flesh, Bellamy made a whimpering sound in his throat. He knew if he saw the wounds in Larry's head he would hurl chunks, so he made sure not to look up. A foul stench was wafting from the body, making Bellamy want to vomit anyway. He fought it as he eased away and settled back onto the recliner.

As he heard footsteps approaching, he slid the gun between his thigh and the chair. Tiffany entered holding her weapon and looking at him with suspicion.

"I thought I heard those chains moving."

"I sneezed. And could you do something about Larry? I can even smell him from over here."

"That's why I went out and got the tarp."

After spreading a blue painter's tarp out beside the sofa, Tiffany managed to roll Larry onto it. The blunt *smack!* the body made upon hitting the plastic was like nothing Bellamy had ever heard before. He feared Tiffany would notice that Larry's holster was empty, but it didn't happen. Larry had settled sideways onto the tarp and was lying on his holster.

Bellamy considered trying to shoot her. However, he knew just enough about guns to know that, although he was only fifteen feet away, he might miss. He hadn't fired a weapon since he used to hunt, during his high school years. No, it was better to bide his time.

Tiffany had also brought in a bundle of blue & white clothesline rope. She went to work on wrapping Larry's corpse and made quite a project out of it. She prattled on as she worked, telling Bellamy about all the things she was going to do once she had the gold.

Her cadence was fast, almost frantic, as caffeine and cocaine fueled her speech. Finally, she finished, and was dragging Larry out the rear door in the kitchen. The going was tough, and she had to rest once; two hundred pounds of dead meat was a lot for a small woman to tug along.

She returned within a few minutes and headed for the sofa. The fresh blood stains at one end of it made her change direction and she plopped down in a chair next to Bellamy.

"I know you're tired," Bellamy said, "But I have to pee."

"Can't it wait?"

"Not really. I haven't gone in a while."

Tiffany released a sigh, dug a key from her pocket, then bent over to unlock the padlocks restricting Bellamy's movement. An instant before Larry's gun smashed the back of her head, she'd flinched, having realized that some of the locks were missing. Tiffany moaned from the blow to her skull but didn't tumble to the floor. Bellamy hit her again, more out of panic than malice. Tiffany fell over, then stopped moving.

Seeing the gash he'd made on her skull and watching the blood seep out was more than he could take. He leaned over and vomited, then felt his strength ebb. Hurting Tiffany was the first violent act Jack Bellamy had ever committed, at least, when he wasn't driving drunk. It sickened him in a way he never would have imagined.

After claiming the key Tiffany dropped, along with her gun, Bellamy shed the chains. Despite the blinds being closed, the sunlight of a new day brightened the room. Bellamy stepped out the front door, took in a deep breath, and inhaled freedom.

26
TICKLED TO DEATH

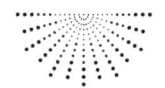

Tanner removed Carl Leffler's body from the freezer and went through the corpse's pockets. Because of the cold, Carl had decomposed very little and still looked like Jack Bellamy.

The most interesting find was a receipt for a hardware store. Bellamy's look-alike had bought chain, padlocks, rope, three shovels, a pickaxe, and three pairs of gloves.

Tanner had passed one of the large warehouse-style hardware stores out on the highway while driving into Byzantine. The only reason he could think of to shop at a small store on the other side of town was because you had additional business in the area. According to the map showing on his phone there were several likely homes in that section. They were all secluded enough to use as a base for a team of kidnappers.

Consulting the tracker revealed that Billy Leffler hadn't budged from his motel room. Tanner was still hopeful that the man would lead him to his friends. However, if he didn't move soon, Tanner faced the choice of abducting him and getting him to talk or searching the area near the hardware store for the gang that took Bellamy.

Whatever he did, he needed to do it soon. It was after seven a.m. and he had a noon deadline. He had never come so close to failing to fulfill a contract, not even before he had become a Tanner. It angered him. In fact, the entire situation was infuriating. Not only were the kidnappers out to get him, but so were the FBI and a corrupt police force. On top of that, he had burned through an alias he had used occasionally for several years. Assets linked and deposited under the Paul Diehl identity would have to be forfeited. That included a small house in Ohio.

Tanner returned to the basement and removed the police uniform from the dryer. It still smelled of smoke, but the odor was faint. When he looked over at the dead body of the look-alike, an idea formed in Tanner's head. Why not let the authorities believe that Bellamy was already dead?

While it wouldn't take the heat off him completely, Tanner thought it should give the FBI and the police the impression that he had left the area. Tanner took out his phone and snapped several photos of the dead body lying on the floor.

∽

Bellamy had dragged Tiffany into the bedroom, stripped her naked, and chained her to the bed.

He knew where he was, after having gone outside and taking a look around. He didn't know the name of the street, but he had spotted the top of the town's tall white water tower off to the west and judged that his home was just eight miles away.

Tiffany's phone had done him no good since the screen was locked with a password. As a lark, he'd typed in COKE WHORE, but apparently, Tiffany had chosen a different password. Larry's phone was with his body, down in a deep hole that Bellamy had seen. Bellamy never seriously considered trying to retrieve the device, not when it meant unwrapping that body down inside a grave.

Tiffany's green Mazda was parked at the rear and Bellamy had the keys in his pocket. Still, he couldn't resist getting revenge before heading out.

A soft moan told him Tiffany was awakening. To help her along, Bellamy splashed whiskey on her face. He had found a bottle in the kitchen and had been drinking the caramel-colored liquid ever since. Some of the fluid had gone up Tiffany's nose and she awoke sputtering.

"Welcome back. As you can see, things have changed."

Tiffany let out another moan. "My head, oh, it hurts, what happened?"

"I clobbered you with a gun—twice."

Tiffany became more aware. She craned her neck forward, looked down along her body, and saw that she was naked and chained spread eagle.

"You sick fuck. You're going to rape me?"

"No, I would never do something like that, nor need to, but I am going to torture you."

Tiffany fought against the chains but soon realized it was no use to struggle.

"Are the police on their way here?"

"I can't call them, unless you want to unlock your phone for me."

"Go to hell."

Bellamy looked her over, pausing to stare at her breasts. "I really did like you."

"You just liked screwing me."

Bellamy laughed. "What else do you have to offer?"

He sat on the bed beside Tiffany and grinned down at her. "Have you ever heard the term, fatal hilarity?"

"It sounds like the name of a band."

"Death from laughter is what it is. I first heard about it when I was living in New York City. I'd gone to see a comedian, and God but the guy was funny. Well, a man sitting three seats away from me was laughing his head off. At one point, I saw that he was as red as an apple and having trouble breathing. The next thing you know, he was dead."

"He had a heart attack?"

"That's what I thought, but no, he died of asphyxiation, you see, he had been laughing so hard he couldn't breathe. I stayed there until a doctor arrived, and that's when I heard the term, fatal hilarity. The poor shmuck laughed himself to death. That's what I've got planned for you."

Tiffany made a face of skepticism. "Even if that was how the man died it had to be a fluke."

"It was the damnedest thing I ever saw, and I want to see it again."

"You really are a sick freak, Jack, which I discovered when we were in bed together."

"I like having my toes licked, so sue me."

"The toes weren't the problem, it was that other thing you wanted me to do, ugh, gross."

"You'd be surprised how many women will do that, and it doesn't hurt to ask."

"I won't laugh myself to death. Besides, there's nothing funny about you."

"You're extremely ticklish. I discovered that about you while we were doing the nasty."

Tiffany went rigid, as she began to suspect what Bellamy had in mind.

"That, that won't kill me, Jack. Why not just leave me here and go away? Let the cops have me."

"I will, but first, let's have some laughs."

Bellamy began tickling Tiffany's right armpit and she attempted to jerk away from him while laughing. Chained to the bed as she was, she couldn't get away, and Bellamy kept at her.

"Torture by tickle," he said, as Tiffany convulsed with laughter. "I may start a trend."

∾

GRANT DIXON WOKE TO FIND THAT HIS UNEXPECTED houseguest was gone. He cursed in frustration. He wanted to speak with Sammy again, as he was hoping to learn the location where Jack Bellamy was being kept.

Where could the boy have gone? Dixon thought, then he wondered if Sammy went back to the Bellamy estate. Dixon hoped that wasn't the case. Sammy might lead the FBI to the kidnappers. If that happened, Jack might be saved. *But no, the boy's ankle was bad. He wouldn't hike back to the estate.*

That thought made him look over at the small table by the door, the one where he placed his keys. They were gone, which meant Sammy had taken his car. Dixon then realized his shotgun was missing as well. *He's gone off to play hero. Damn it!*

∾

BELLAMY TICKLED TIFFANY WITHOUT CEASING UNTIL SHE was red in the face and her breath was catching in her throat. He stopped and backed away from the bed, after Tiffany wet the sheets.

"Oh, that's nasty."

"It's your fault, you idiot. I couldn't help it."

Bellamy picked up Larry's gun and pointed it at Tiffany. "Tickling you to death won't work, but I bet you'll die if I pull this—" Bellamy stopped talking when he heard a sound behind him. He turned his head to look and saw the butt of a shotgun heading toward his face. After that, it was lights out.

∾

SAMMY WATCHED HIS BROTHER FALL TO THE CARPET, THEN looked over at Tiffany. "I can't believe Jack was going to kill you."

Tiffany was staring at Sammy with her mouth hanging open. She had received a message earlier from Melissa saying that Sammy was dead. After recovering from the shock of seeing him alive, she spoke to him.

"Get these chains off me, Sammy."

Sammy was staring at her, taking in her naked body, while paying particular attention to the area between her spread legs.

"Sammy!"

His eyes shot to her face. "Sorry, but wow, you're beautiful."

"Remove these damn chains before Jack wakes up."

Sammy leaned back against a dresser to take weight off his bad ankle.

"I snuck up on the house from the rear. I saw the grave. Who is wrapped inside the tarp, Tiffany?"

"That's Larry. Your brother killed him, and he would have killed me too."

Sammy stared down at Jack. A lump was beginning to rise on Bellamy's forehead, and he was still unconscious.

"Jack killed Larry? How did that happen?"

"He's a tricky bastard, you know that. Now, Sammy, please, free me from this bed. Jack might have the key in his pocket."

Sammy placed the shotgun on the dresser before limping over to a nightstand. "This looks like a padlock key."

When Tiffany was free, she put her arms around Sammy's neck and kissed him. "My hero."

Being only nineteen and having a naked woman press herself against him caused Sammy to have a predictable reaction. It didn't go unnoticed by Tiffany, who had known her kiss would have that effect on him. As she was getting into a robe, Tiffany smiled at Sammy.

"I'll show you just how grateful I am later. Right now, we have to get Jack secured. Help me carry him into the living room."

"What are you going to do to him?"

"I'm going to chain him back in the chair where he was."

"I won't let you kill him, Tiffany."

"What? I don't want to kill Jack. And even if I did, you know we need him alive until that clause in Melissa's prenuptial agreement kicks in at midnight."

"Don't trust Melissa, she tried to have me killed."

"Are you serious?"

"Hell yeah, two guys tossed me off a cliff last night. I'm lucky I survived with just a bad ankle."

Tiffany touched Sammy on the cheek while looking at him with sympathy. "You poor thing. I don't know why she would do that. Are you sure she was behind it?"

"No one else knew I would be there."

Tiffany leaned over to grab Bellamy by the ankles, then straightened up and moaned. "Ow, before I do anything I have to take something for this headache. Yell for me if Jack begins to wake up."

"I will, but I hit him pretty hard. I hope I didn't hurt him too bad."

Tiffany disappeared into the adjacent bathroom and Sammy heard water running. He figured he could handle Jack alone and dragged him into the living room. After grabbing him beneath his arms, Sammy hefted Jack up and sat him in the recliner. As he was puzzling over the hole in the ceiling, Tiffany called to him.

"Give me a few more minutes, Sammy. I need to take a shower."

"All right, I can handle Jack."

Sammy chained his brother to the recliner again while Tiffany showered. After the water shut off in the bathroom, Sammy heard a loud sniff. Along with pain reliever, Tiffany was medicating with cocaine. She appeared in the doorway moments later, naked, clean, and with a smile on her beautiful face.

"Is he still out?" Tiffany asked.

"Yeah, but I think he's starting to come around."

"I see you chained him to the chair, that's good."

"Uh-huh," Sammy said, as he stared at Tiffany.

"Do you like what you see, Sammy?"

"Oh yeah."

Tiffany turned in the doorway and sent a sultry smile over her shoulder. "Come in the bedroom and I'll reward you for saving me."

Sammy watched Tiffany leave the doorway. He limped toward the room as fast as he could, entered it, and saw no one.

"Tiffany?"

Assuming she must have gone back into the bathroom, Sammy went in, but she wasn't there either. As he turned to walk back out of the bathroom, he spotted her. Tiffany had been ducked down out of sight on the other side of the bed. She was on the floor, sitting up on her knees, and the shotgun was propped on the mattress. The Benelli spat fire as death left its barrel. Sammy took the blast to the chest and stumbled backwards to land inside the bathtub.

Tiffany ran into the room to look at him and saw a pair of lifeless blue eyes staring up at her. After snorting more coke and getting dressed quickly, she went into the living room. In her hands was the shotgun. Bellamy was awake, but he looked confused and groggy.

"What was that noise?"

"I killed Sammy."

"Sammy? Was he a part of this too?"

"Melissa seduced him into it."

"You know my wife?"

"This kidnapping plan was all hers, so you couldn't divorce her before your third anniversary."

"What an evil bitch."

"She's not evil, Jack. Melissa just outsmarted you."

Bellamy shut his eyes against a wave of pain. "I've got one hell of a headache. Who hit me?"

"Sammy did."

"Then fuck him, the ungrateful asshole."

Tiffany's large, dilated pupils stared into Bellamy's eyes. "Tell me where I can find the gold."

Bellamy studied Tiffany's face, looked at the shotgun, and told her what she wanted to hear.

27
THE WIDOW BELLAMY

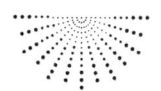

Tanner was searching the area where he suspected Bellamy was being held captive. The homes in the region were separated by large tracts of undeveloped land and the roads were few and narrow.

He had donned the police uniform again and was driving the old Chevy Cavalier. If he were spotted by a resident of the area he would claim to be an off-duty cop looking for the home of a friend. However, few cars were on the road since it was a Sunday.

Before leaving the bungalow, Tanner had sent off the photos he'd taken of the corpse. Melissa Bellamy had engineered her husband's kidnapping to keep him from cutting her off from a scheduled windfall. If Bellamy divorced her or died, she would get nothing. Tanner wondered what Melissa Bellamy's reaction would be once she was told her husband was dead.

Melissa felt her knees give out. If Agent Willis hadn't grabbed her arm and supported her, she would have collapsed to the living room floor.

"Are you certain he's dead?"

"Yes, ma'am, and we're so sorry. A photo was sent to us. The kidnappers claim that they're cutting their losses and have left the area. I want you to know that this isn't over. The FBI will do everything in its power to track these people down."

A great sob fueled by grief and loss erupted from Melissa. The emotions were as real as the tears they had given birth to. Melissa Bellamy was grieving over the loss of millions that had been only hours away from becoming a reality. She had spent three years being the wife of Jack Bellamy, three long years. There had to be a payoff. It couldn't have all been for nothing.

Peter Fairfax came over to Melissa and put an arm around her shoulders. He looked every bit the avuncular family friend and trusted advisor he claimed to be.

"Gentlemen, ladies, I'm going to escort Mrs. Bellamy to her room to rest. I'm sure you'll understand."

Agent Willis and Agent Williams nodded along with the others present and told Melissa how sorry they were for her loss.

Only one man said nothing. That was Chief Greene. Bellamy's death meant that his secret would be revealed for everyone to see. As far as the chief was concerned, his life had ended as well. He sat slumped in a loveseat, alone, with an empty look in his eyes.

~

After leading her up the staircase and opening her bedroom door for her, Fairfax followed Melissa inside.

Melissa was still dazed by the turn of events, but not so much that she didn't notice that she was alone in a locked bedroom with Fairfax.

"You can leave now, Peter; I'll be fine."

Fairfax smiled at her, walked over to the bed, and laid back upon it.

"I'd rather stay. We need to talk."

Melissa was shocked by his boldness, then she brightened as a thought occurred to her.

"Jack's will. Did he leave me anything in it?"

"He did indeed."

"How much?"

"Nine dollars."

"Nine... dollars?"

"On the video will he left behind, he says you were a perfect ten when he married you, but that you've drifted down into the nine tier, thus the nine dollars."

"I hope that's a joke."

"You knew the man; you tell me."

Melissa balled her hands into fists and released a howl of rage. "That bastard!"

"That he was," Fairfax agreed.

Melissa settled on the side of the bed with her head hung low. "I was so close to getting three million dollars, you know, as per the terms of our prenuptial agreement."

"Actually, you weren't. At my insistence, Jack filed divorce papers on Thursday. He was planning to serve you himself tomorrow. By filing, he nullified your agreement."

Melissa stood and glared at Fairfax. "This is why you've had that damn smile on your face. You're as sadistic as Jack."

"That was one reason for my smile, the other being that I knew all about your plans to kidnap him."

Melissa tried to laugh, but it sounded more like she was wheezing.

"You can't be serious. You think I had something to do with that?"

"I don't think it; I know it. I'm also aware that an accomplice of yours named Carl was killed while pretending to be Jack. The others are named Rudy, Larry, Tiffany, and let's not forget Sammy. By the way, I haven't seen the young man and he's not in his room above the garage."

Melissa broke eye contact as she said, "I don't know where Sammy is... how did you find out about the kidnapping?"

Fairfax pointed a finger up at the light fixture in the ceiling. "I placed a camera up there some time ago."

"You... what?"

"The device is small, but the picture and sound quality are excellent."

Melissa made a face of disgust. "You've seen me naked? You've watched me in bed with Jack?"

"With Jack, with Sammy, that young man who works with the lawn service, a delivery man, and three other men I never identified. It was all quite entertaining."

"You're a sick old bastard."

"If so, I'm a sick old bastard that could put you behind bars for many years."

"You've filmed Sammy and me talking about the kidnapping?"

"I did, several times. There's just one thing I don't understand."

"What's that?"

"This man who came here earlier pretending to be a police officer, who was he, another accomplice?"

"He was a hit man to kill Jack... did you hire him?"

"Me? No, Melissa. I knew that Jack was never going to survive his kidnapping, and he didn't."

"None of my friends killed him, not before the deadline. The hit man must have murdered Jack... and everyone else. I haven't heard back from Tiffany, Larry, or the Leffler brothers."

"Who are the Leffler brothers?"

"They're Carl's cousins. They came here to kill the hit man, but I guess he got to them first."

Fairfax patted the bed. "Come lie next to me."

"In your dreams."

"I won't deny that I dream about you. Let me put it this way, lie next to me, or else."

Melissa's shoulders slumped. "You're going to blackmail me for sex?"

"That's a crude way of putting it, but I'd also like to marry you, after a respectable mourning period."

"You're forty years older than me."

"I'm also rich."

"How rich, as rich as Jack?"

"No, but I am a millionaire many times over."

Melissa stared at Fairfax through hooded eyes. After sighing in resignation, she climbed up onto the bed and lay beside him, as he placed an arm around her.

"I suppose you want me to screw you now?"

"Tomorrow would be better for me, dear. As you said, I'm an old man, and I barely slept a wink last night. But don't worry, I'll be ready, willing, and able, that is, after I get some sleep."

"Don't rush on my account."

Fairfax laughed, leaned over, and kissed Melissa. Although she made a face of disgust, he was smiling.

"Peter, who did Jack leave his money to?"

"He left the estate, his money, and his other holdings to his first wife. He said she loved him when he had nothing."

"Isn't she in a mental institution?"

"Yes, Jack drove her crazy."

"Then what happens to the money?"

"Everything will be kept in a trust and handled by her lawyer, who has her power of attorney."

Melissa shifted until she was lying on her side and facing Fairfax. "That lawyer is you, isn't it?"

"Yes, quite a coincidence, wouldn't you say?"

Melissa smiled, then laughed.

"Peter."

"Hmm?"

Melissa snuggled up against him. "Maybe life with you won't be so bad after all."

Fairfax didn't answer. The old man had fallen asleep.

28
SECRET REVEALED

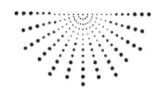

Chief of Police Martin Greene was inside the Byzantine bank making a withdrawal. With him was the bank's branch manager, Carol Miller. Mrs. Miller was wearing pajamas and slippers. Chief Greene was wearing a ski mask and a jogging outfit.

The chief had broken into the branch manager's home and roused her and her husband from a sound sleep. After handcuffing the husband to a pipe in the basement, Greene forced the branch manager to accompany him to the bank.

Greene was aware that the time lock on the bank vault was broken and had yet to be repaired. He also knew there was over a hundred thousand sitting in the safe. He was going to take it to fund his new life. He believed that Bellamy was dead. That meant at some point over the next few days an email would be automatically sent from an unknown account.

Dozens, if not hundreds of people would receive photos that Bellamy had taken of the chief, photos that would ruin him and make his life a living hell. Before that event took place, Greene was going to be in the wind.

With the money secured in a laptop bag, Greene dealt with the bank manager. He locked the woman inside her own vault, after disabling the emergency phone it contained. After waiting until a car drove past, he left the bank and headed for the vehicle he had taken from the impound lot.

He was a block from the bank and reaching up to take off his mask when he spotted the flashing lights in his mirror. After fumbling with the hand-held scanner he'd brought along, he learned that his men knew about the bank robbery. Greene pressed down harder on the gas pedal as he tried to evade his own officers.

~

THE CHIEF SHOULD HAVE PAID MORE ATTENTION TO THE spot he had chosen to place the branch manager's husband. The basement pipe the man had been handcuffed to was near a drawer that contained hacksaw blades. The man cut through the copper pipe he was secured to, slid the cuff free, and ran upstairs to get his phone.

~

CHIEF GREENE SLAMMED INTO A METAL FENCE POST AFTER rounding a curve and nearly ran head on into a tractor-trailer. The driver of the big rig blew his air horn and kept going. The car stalled as the airbag deployed, and Greene bailed out.

The fence he had collided with bordered tracks that

were used by slow-moving freight trains originating from the south in Williamson. One such train was approaching with dozens of coal cars attached. Chief Greene knew if he could reach it he might be able to escape pursuit by climbing aboard.

It would be even better if he could make it across the tracks before the train arrived. As slow as the locomotive was moving, he'd be through the woods and in the next town before anyone could follow on foot.

Greene started up the fence and found the going tough. He was in his fifties and hadn't climbed anything other than stairs since he was a boy. His feet were finding purchase in the chain-links, but he barely had the strength to pull himself up.

After reaching the top of the fence he straddled it briefly to catch his breath, as the pointy metal prongs dug into his thighs. When he looked to see how close his pursuers were, he was startled. He had three patrol cars after him, and they were only seconds behind him.

The hand holding the laptop bag slipped, causing Greene to slice open his palm and lose his balance. His full weight dropped onto the tips of the fence and he felt the flesh of his thighs being punctured in several places. Then, he was falling. Greene managed to get the fingers of his left hand around several chain links, which kept him from plunging the twelve feet to the ground.

Instead, he flipped over and smashed backwards against the fence. The one-handed grip couldn't hold his weight. The chief completed his fall to the ground, where he landed on his stomach. His pants and the boxers beneath them had been torn open at the crotch and the backs of his thighs were bleeding.

Greene, while moaning in panic and pain, lifted

himself up off the grass. After he reclaimed his dropped bag of loot, the chief dashed toward the tracks. With his pants ripped open, he felt the breeze on his balls. It was an odd sensation.

Behind him came the clanging of the fence as multiple men scaled it. They were men decades younger and pounds lighter than Greene. The slowest of them made it over the barrier in four seconds.

"Stop shithead or I'll shoot!"

Greene recognized the voice. It was an officer named Clay Darrow. Officer Darrow was known to be a good shot. Nevertheless, his first two rounds missed wide as the tracks grew closer. Officer Clay Darrow's next three shots did not miss. Chief Greene lived long enough to see a piece of his heart get blown out of his chest before his body fell onto the gravel that lined the railroad tracks.

There had been five cops in the three cars that pursued Greene. They gathered around the body as the freight train rumbled slowly past.

One of the men yanked the mask off Greene's face and cursed in surprise. "It's Chief Greene. The son of a bitch robbed the bank."

One of the other men pointed down along Greene's body, where his crotch was exposed. He was laughing. "Yo, Clay, you shot the chief's damn dick off."

"No, I didn't, Eddie. My shots hit him in the back."

"Then where's his wiener?"

Clay Darrow leaned closer. "Oh man. Will you look at that? Is that the smallest prick you've ever seen or what?"

"My two-year-old has got a bigger one," Eddie said.

The men had a good laugh over the chief's… shortcoming, and they snapped a few pictures to pass around. Afterward, their attention turned to the bank money. They decided they would split it up five ways and report that Chief Greene's "unknown accomplice" escaped with the cash. The decision to keep the money was a no-brainer for Byzantine's finest.

29

HORRIBLY DISAPPOINTED

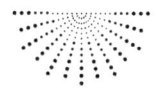

Tanner was moving his car along the driveway of a home he had checked for signs of the kidnappers. The house had been sitting empty and was up for sale. It was the third such home he'd investigated while searching for Bellamy. Another property had been occupied by a family who were loading up their car, as if headed out for the day.

It was after nine a.m. and the deadline was looming. With eleven more homes to check out, Tanner was feeling the pressure. It was an odd sensation to be on edge and one Tanner didn't like. Still, not for one instant did he think he would fail. Such thoughts were never allowed to enter his mind.

Stopping halfway down the driveway, Tanner paused to review the location of the tracker he'd placed on Billy Leffler's Escalade. Not only had the vehicle been on the move since he last checked it, but it was stopped only a few miles away.

BILLY HAD ARRIVED AT THE HOME WHERE BELLAMY WAS being held and was met outside by Tiffany. She was holding the Benelli shotgun she used to kill Sammy, but she kept the barrel pointed toward the ground.

"How did you know where I was?" she asked Billy.

He looked at her with bloodshot eyes. "Joe's dead. He was killed by that hit man."

"Damn, Billy. I'm sorry, but listen, you can't stay here. You don't want Bellamy to see you, do you?"

"What's it matter? I know you plan to kill him. Joe and I spotted that grave behind the house when we followed you here last night."

"Um, plans have changed. I'm going to keep him alive and try to collect the ransom."

"That's risky, ain't it?"

"It is, and that's why you don't want any part of it."

Bellamy shouted from inside the house. "Who's out there?"

"You don't need to know that, Jack," Tiffany said.

"Hey, whoever you are, did she tell you about the gold?"

Tiffany gritted her teeth, then turned it into a smile. "Don't pay any attention to him, Billy. He suffered a blow to the head and has been babbling since it happened."

Billy glared at Tiffany with narrowed eyes and pushed past her. When he walked over to Bellamy, who was chained to the recliner, the former hedge fund manager smiled up at him.

"I hope you're not one of Tiffany's partners; she has a nasty habit of killing them."

Bellamy tossed his head toward the sofa, indicating the blood stains soaking into the cushions.

Billy spun around and grabbed the shotgun out of Tiffany's hands.

"I was just holding it," she said.

"Yeah, well now I'm holding it, and what's this about gold?"

"Tiffany and I made a deal. She doesn't kill me, and I tell her where to find gold that I buried."

"Is it a lot of gold?"

"Millions, my friend, it's millions in gold."

"I want in on that," Billy said.

Tiffany waved a dismissive hand at Bellamy. "It's all a lie, Billy. It's a lie he made up to try to save his life."

"There's an easy way to find out. Let's make him take us to the gold."

"He might try to escape."

Billy's right hand shot out and he gave Bellamy's face two hard slaps, one with the palm, and the other backhanded.

"You're not going to try to escape, are you, buddy?"

Bellamy shook his head, as a trickle of blood leaked from the corner of his mouth. "I wouldn't dream of it."

Tiffany turned and headed for the door. "Let's talk about this where Jack can't hear us."

Billy followed her outside and they walked past the Escalade.

⁓

Inside the home, Bellamy could hear Tiffany and Billy talking but couldn't make out their words. He struggled against the chains and got nowhere.

"Psst!"

Bellamy heard the whispered sound come from behind him and turned his head to see Grant Dixon peeking around the corner of the kitchen doorway. Sammy had arrived in the area after taking Dixon's Mercedes and shotgun. Dixon found the house by having his car's location tracked through the vehicle recovery system installed in his Mercedes. To get there, he had driven his other vehicle, a black 2001 Camaro SS.

Had Tiffany not been fueled by cocaine and caffeine she might have had the good sense to find Dixon's Mercedes and move it. Fortunately for Bellamy, the thought never occurred to her and she just assumed that Sammy had driven there in his own vehicle.

Dixon whispered to Bellamy. "Are those two outside the only ones here?"

Bellamy whispered back through a huge grin. "Yeah, get me out of here, Dix."

Dixon walked over to the chair in a crouch, as outside, Tiffany and Billy's conversation became louder. Dixon carried a handgun and was dressed in jeans and a long-sleeve T-shirt.

Tiffany had left the key to the padlocks on the fireplace mantel. Once Dixon had it, he went to work opening the padlocks. He frowned when he saw the purplish swelling on Bellamy's forehead.

"That's a nasty lump you got there?"

"I have Sammy to thank for it."

"Where is Sammy, Jack?"

"Dead."

"Shit."

"Fuck him; he helped kidnap me."

The words, "There is no gold, it's all a lie!" came from outside as Tiffany raised her voice.

Dixon shook his head as a smile crept over his lips. "Don't tell me you used that old gold scam again?"

"It still works."

"You had half the guys in the fraternity digging up the

campus looking for your bogus gold. How much did you say you buried this time?"

Bellamy's eyes twinkled. "Millions, millions in gold."

Dixon stifled a laugh. Bellamy always could make him smile. Then, he remembered the treachery that his friend was planning.

"I know, Jack."

"You know what?"

"About the interview you have scheduled. Do you have any idea what that would do to me?"

"It's not all about you, Dix. I want recognition. I want my reputation back."

"They'll toss your ass in prison this time for violating your agreement. I'll be sent there too for helping you."

"I'll make it work, you'll see," Bellamy said.

Dixon removed another padlock and the final chain holding Bellamy grew slack. Bellamy eased out of the recliner and stood. Free again.

He smiled at Dixon, who was standing a few feet away on his right, but the grin died as Bellamy felt his blood run cold. The look in his old friend's eyes was like nothing he'd ever seen before. The man was also pointing his gun at his chest.

"I won't let you ruin me, Jack."

"Hey, Dix."

"What?"

"They've stopped talking outside."

One of the front windows exploded, as outside Billy fired the shotgun through the glass. The blast entered the rear of Grant Dixon's head and removed his face. Some of the gore splattered Bellamy's right sleeve and soaked through to touch his skin.

The shock of watching his friend die froze Bellamy long enough for Billy and Tiffany to enter. Billy was laughing, and when he walked over to Dixon's body he spat on it.

"That's the fucker who killed Joe."

"Are you sure?" Tiffany said.

"I never got a good look at him, but he was about to blow Bellamy here to hell."

"But why did he free him from the chair first? That seems like he was trying to help him escape."

"Bellamy," Billy said. "Did you know this man?"

Bellamy recalled the look he'd seen in his old friend's eyes, and the way his finger had been poised to pull the trigger.

"No, I never knew him."

Tiffany pointed down at the body with a puzzled expression. "What's that around his neck?"

"Where?" Billy said, as he leaned over to get a better look.

If the snap on Tiffany's holster hadn't been so loud, Billy might have joined Dixon on the floor. He jerked his head around to see Tiffany pulling out her weapon, then pivoted with the shotgun. Tiffany's first round caught Billy high on the left side of his chest. As his shotgun went off at close range, her second round struck Billy's shoulder.

Tiffany dropped to her knees, her mouth and eyes opened wide in shocked realization of her impending death. Tiffany had a hole in her stomach that Bellamy could see through.

"Oh, sweet Jesus," Bellamy said.

Tiffany's dilated pupils shrunk down to the size of pinpricks before she toppled backward onto the carpet to die.

Bellamy spun around and bolted for the rear door in the kitchen. After gathering himself and taking a quick assessment of his wounds, Billy followed him outside. He was dripping blood all the way.

∽

I SHOULD HAVE WORKED OUT, I SHOULD HAVE WORKED OUT, Bellamy thought as he ran along beneath a canopy of trees. He had covered only a hundred yards and was panting and sweating.

When he heard Billy shout for him to stop, Bellamy was amazed at how near the voice was. He risked a glance backwards, tripped over a vine, and went sprawling.

The sound of old leaves crunching underfoot came closer. Bellamy crawled over to a tree and rested his back against it while taking in deep breaths. Billy, shotgun poised to fire, came closer and towered over him. Billy's left side was streaked with blood and rage filled his eyes.

"Don't shoot me, there really is gold... really," Bellamy said.

The shot was loud. Bellamy thought Billy had fired the shotgun, that is, until he looked up and saw the entry hole in Billy's forehead. The body swayed, then tipped over like a falling tree. The crunch of leaves came from behind Bellamy this time, and he swiveled around.

There was a policeman walking toward him, and damn if the guy didn't have a serious set of eyes. Bellamy smiled in greeting and released a laugh, as relief flooded him. He was certain he was being rescued from his ordeal. However, that was no policeman. It was Tanner.

Jack Bellamy was about to be horribly disappointed.

30
SUGAR AND SPICE, AND EVERYTHING NICE

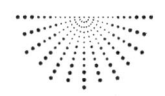

Following an anonymous tip, the FBI arrived at the kidnapper's hideout and came across the bodies of Jack Bellamy and several others. When the coroner stated that Bellamy had been dead for less than an hour, Agents Williams and Willis puzzled over that fact. How had they received a photo of Bellamy's body before the man had died?

That question would be answered the following day when they were again informed anonymously about another crime scene. Once there, the body of Carl Leffler, makeup and all, would be discovered stuffed inside a freezer.

~

Tanner didn't tip the FBI about Bellamy's love nest until the next day because he had decided to use it again. He knew the search would be on for anyone involved in the kidnapping and murders. There was also a manhunt underway for an accomplice of the late Chief Greene.

According to the first officers on the scene, an unknown white male of average height and build was seen in the passenger seat of the chief's getaway car. That same man somehow avoided capture. He was said to have gotten away with over a hundred thousand dollars.

With so much going on and having not slept and barely eaten for more than a day, Tanner decided to rest and stay off the streets. He did just that, while also enjoying a good meal. He was more than ready to leave town the following morning. Before exiting the bungalow, Tanner spent a little time on the internet. There were a couple of loose ends that needed snipping.

~

AT THE BELLAMY ESTATE, THE RECENTLY WIDOWED Melissa Bellamy was about to climb into bed with Peter Fairfax. Fairfax was rested, ready, and had taken a little blue pill that would ensure he remained virile.

Melissa had sweated out the previous day after her friends and fellow kidnappers were found dead.

When the FBI claimed that the group had apparently had a fatal falling out, she wondered how it had all transpired. Then came the news that Jack's friend Grant Dixon was somehow involved. How and why Dixon came to be at the house where Jack was being held, Melissa couldn't even guess.

Late in the day, word arrived that the crime scene had been processed, although the investigation would continue. There was still the matter of identifying and apprehending the man who had entered the Bellamy home on the previous evening.

Melissa was no longer afraid Tanner would come after her. Now that her husband was dead, and his contract fulfilled, he would have no reason to trouble her. She alone survived the death and mayhem that the kidnapping had spawned. And while it was true she stood to inherit nothing —other than nine dollars—her lifestyle would remain the same.

Peter Fairfax would have control of the estate, and he had told Melissa that she could live there as long as she kept him happy. If she ever failed to do so, she would find herself in a very uncomfortable position.

Melissa smiled at Fairfax as she stood beside the bed in a white lace negligee. She had resigned herself to becoming the devious old man's paramour. Given time, she was certain she would think of a way to beat him at his own game.

"What are all those sounds coming from outside?" Fairfax asked.

"Those are news vans, over a dozen of them are parked at the gates."

"I thought they would go away now that the kidnapping was over."

"Apparently not," Melissa said.

Fairfax held out a hand. "Join me, my dear."

Melissa removed the negligee and slid onto the bed. Fairfax looked down along the sensuous body of a woman he lusted after for years, as he trembled with anticipation.

"I've waited for this moment since I first laid eyes on you, Melissa."

A loud splintering sound came from downstairs as the front door was busted open by a battering ram. That was followed by a voice shouting orders and another calling Melissa's name.

Melissa and Fairfax looked at each other with stunned expressions as the thump of pounding feet ran up the stairs. When the bedroom door was shoved open,

Melissa found herself staring at FBI Special Agents Williams and Willis. With them were a number of heavily-armed federal agents. More men and women could be heard moving from room to room throughout the house.

"We've located both subjects upstairs," Williams said into a radio.

Melissa and Fairfax were yanked from the bed and made to lie atop the floor on their stomachs. After their hands were cuffed behind them, they were covered up by robes, a pair of which had been draped over a chair.

"What the hell is going on?" Melissa asked. When she turned her head to look, she saw Agent Williams using the foot board as a step ladder, to reach up toward the ceiling.

"Here it is," Williams said.

Melissa watched her remove, or was Williams a man? Melissa still couldn't tell the agents apart, but she watched as Williams removed a small object. The white round disc had been magnetically attached to one of the overhead ceiling vents and had blended in well. Melissa was puzzled as she tried to figure out what it was, but Fairfax knew.

"Oh no," the old man said.

"What is it, Peter?"

"It's a camera," Agent Williams said.

Melissa looked over at Fairfax. "Peter?"

"It's not mine, dear. I don't know who placed it there."

"It was first activated in the late morning two days ago, or so we were told in an anonymous phone call," Williams said. "It recorded whenever there was motion detected."

"Late morning, two days ago?" Melissa said, and she remembered Tanner had first confronted her at that time.

"When you say it activated, do you mean that device recorded conversations in this room?"

"That's correct, Mr. Fairfax," Agent Willis said, "and

we have the interesting ones you and Mrs. Bellamy have had."

Melissa shed tears as she recalled the things they had said. Her culpability in the kidnapping would be obvious to anyone. Fairfax was also in trouble, as he admitted having foreknowledge of abduction and murder.

"It doesn't matter what was recorded," Fairfax said. "Any decent defense attorney would have it thrown out of court."

"Maybe, maybe not," Williams said. "But that same lawyer will have quite a time finding a potential juror who doesn't know about the video. Whoever planted the camera downloaded the conversations you two had on the internet."

"That was done before we were told about it," Agent Willis said. "They've gone viral, which is why all the news vans are back outside."

Melissa shed more tears, and Fairfax joined in on the weeping, but for a different reason.

"Couldn't you have come an hour later?" Fairfax whined. "Oh, I was so close to finally having her, so close."

Williams nodded at the other agents, and the pair was carted away.

∼

TANNER DROVE THE STREETS OF BYZANTINE FOR THE FINAL time while cruising along in Carl Leffler's vehicle. The car was a white 2010 Mini Cooper. The sporty BMW had been inside the bungalow's detached garage and had a full tank of gas.

Tanner had never been so happy to leave a town before and couldn't wait to get back home to Sara. And yet, after seeing a familiar sight, he decided to make one last stop.

The little blonde girl radiated gratitude when Tanner offered to get her kitten out of a tree. Once he had the feline and handed it to her, she beamed up at him with a sweet smile.

"Thank you, mister."

"You're welcome, honey, but maybe you should keep your kitten indoors. It's safer."

"Okay."

Tanner returned to the Mini, and within minutes he was finally free of the town of Byzantine. With his fake ID compromised, he couldn't fly home, so he'd decided to drive the five-hundred miles. When he stopped for gas in rural Pennsylvania, he discovered his wallet was missing, and that he'd become a victim of Byzantine's notorious pickpocket. But how? He hadn't been near anyone except…

"The little girl with the kitten."

She must have removed his wallet while his back was turned, and he was reaching up to grab her cat. Tanner sat in the car laughing, while vowing to never again set foot in the corrupt town of Byzantine.

TANNER RETURNS!

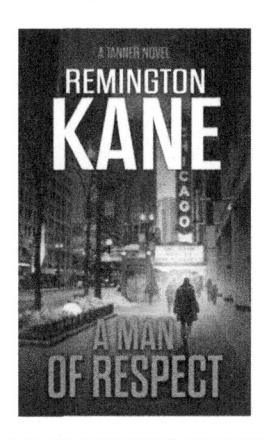

A MAN OF RESPECT - TANNER 23

AFTERWORD

Thank you,

REMINGTON KANE

JOIN MY INNER CIRCLE

You'll receive FREE books, such as,

SLAY BELLS – A TANNER NOVEL – BOOK 0

TAKEN! ALPHABET SERIES – 26 ORIGINAL TAKEN! TALES

BLUE STEELE - KARMA

Also – Exclusive short stories featuring TANNER, along with other books.

TO BECOME AN INNER CIRCLE MEMBER, GO TO:

http://remingtonkane.com/mailing-list/

ALSO BY REMINGTON KANE

The TANNER Series in order

INEVITABLE I - A Tanner Novel - Book 1

KILL IN PLAIN SIGHT - A Tanner Novel - Book 2

MAKING A KILLING ON WALL STREET - A Tanner Novel - Book 3

THE FIRST ONE TO DIE LOSES - A Tanner Novel - Book 4

THE LIFE & DEATH OF CODY PARKER - A Tanner Novel - Book 5

WAR - A Tanner Novel- A Tanner Novel - Book 6

SUICIDE OR DEATH - A Tanner Novel - Book 7

TWO FOR THE KILL - A Tanner Novel - Book 8

BALLET OF DEATH - A Tanner Novel - Book 9

MORE DANGEROUS THAN MAN - A Tanner Novel - Book 10

TANNER TIMES TWO - A Tanner Novel - Book 11

OCCUPATION: DEATH - A Tanner Novel - Book 12

HELL FOR HIRE - A Tanner Novel - Book 13

A HOME TO DIE FOR - A Tanner Novel - Book 14

FIRE WITH FIRE - A Tanner Novel - Book 15

TO KILL A KILLER - A Tanner Novel - Book 16

WHITE HELL – A Tanner Novel - Book 17

MANHATTAN HIT MAN – A Tanner Novel - Book 18

ONE HUNDRED YEARS OF TANNER – A Tanner Novel -

Book 19

REVELATIONS - A Tanner Novel - Book 20

THE SPY GAME - A Tanner Novel - Book 21

A VICTIM OF CIRCUMSTANCE - A Tanner Novel - Book 22

A MAN OF RESPECT - A Tanner Novel - Book 23

THE MAN, THE MYTH - A Tanner Novel - Book 24

ALL-OUT WAR - A Tanner Novel - Book 25

THE REAL DEAL - A Tanner Novel - Book 26

WAR ZONE - A Tanner Novel - Book 27

ULTIMATE ASSASSIN - A Tanner Novel - Book 28

KNIGHT TIME - A Tanner Novel - Book 29

PROTECTOR - A Tanner Novel - Book 30

BULLETS BEFORE BREAKFAST - A Tanner Novel - Book 31

VENGEANCE - A Tanner Novel - Book 32

TARGET: TANNER - A Tanner Novel - Book 33

BLACK SHEEP - A Tanner Novel - Book 34

FLESH AND BLOOD - A Tanner Novel - Book 35

NEVER SEE IT COMING - A Tanner Novel - Book 36

MISSING - A Tanner Novel - Book 37

CONTENDER - A Tanner Novel - Book 38

TO SERVE AND PROTECT - A Tanner Novel - Book 39

STALKING HORSE - A Tanner Novel - Book 40

THE EVIL OF TWO LESSERS - A Tanner Novel - Book 41

SINS OF THE FATHER AND MOTHER - A Tanner Novel - Book 42

SOULLESS - A Tanner Novel - Book 43

The Young Guns Series in order

YOUNG GUNS
YOUNG GUNS 2 - SMOKE & MIRRORS
YOUNG GUNS 3 - BEYOND LIMITS
YOUNG GUNS 4 - RYKER'S RAIDERS
YOUNG GUNS 5 - ULTIMATE TRAINING
YOUNG GUNS 6 - CONTRACT TO KILL
YOUNG GUNS 7 - FIRST LOVE
YOUNG GUNS 8 - THE END OF THE BEGINNING

A Tanner Series in order

TANNER: YEAR ONE
TANNER: YEAR TWO
TANNER: YEAR THREE
TANNER: YEAR FOUR
TANNER: YEAR FIVE

The TAKEN! Series in order

TAKEN! - LOVE CONQUERS ALL - Book 1
TAKEN! - SECRETS & LIES - Book 2
TAKEN! - STALKER - Book 3
TAKEN! - BREAKOUT! - Book 4
TAKEN! - THE THIRTY-NINE - Book 5
TAKEN! - KIDNAPPING THE DEVIL - Book 6
TAKEN! - HIT SQUAD - Book 7
TAKEN! - MASQUERADE - Book 8

TAKEN! - SERIOUS BUSINESS - Book 9

TAKEN! - THE COUPLE THAT SLAYS TOGETHER - Book 10

TAKEN! - PUT ASUNDER - Book 11

TAKEN! - LIKE BOND, ONLY BETTER - Book 12

TAKEN! - MEDIEVAL - Book 13

TAKEN! - RISEN! - Book 14

TAKEN! - VACATION - Book 15

TAKEN! - MICHAEL - Book 16

TAKEN! - BEDEVILED - Book 17

TAKEN! - INTENTIONAL ACTS OF VIOLENCE - Book 18

TAKEN! - THE KING OF KILLERS – Book 19

TAKEN! - NO MORE MR. NICE GUY - Book 20 & the Series Finale

The MR. WHITE Series

PAST IMPERFECT - MR. WHITE - Book 1

HUNTED - MR. WHITE - Book 2

The BLUE STEELE Series in order

BLUE STEELE - BOUNTY HUNTER- Book 1

BLUE STEELE - BROKEN- Book 2

BLUE STEELE - VENGEANCE- Book 3

BLUE STEELE - THAT WHICH DOESN'T KILL ME- Book 4

BLUE STEELE - ON THE HUNT- Book 5

BLUE STEELE - PAST SINS - Book 6

BLUE STEELE - DADDY'S GIRL - Book 7 & the Series Finale

The CALIBER DETECTIVE AGENCY Series in order

CALIBER DETECTIVE AGENCY - GENERATIONS- Book 1

CALIBER DETECTIVE AGENCY - TEMPTATION- Book 2

CALIBER DETECTIVE AGENCY - A RANSOM PAID IN BLOOD- Book 3

CALIBER DETECTIVE AGENCY - MISSING- Book 4

CALIBER DETECTIVE AGENCY - DECEPTION- Book 5

CALIBER DETECTIVE AGENCY - CRUCIBLE- Book 6

CALIBER DETECTIVE AGENCY – LEGENDARY – Book 7

CALIBER DETECTIVE AGENCY – WE ARE GATHERED HERE TODAY - Book 8

CALIBER DETECTIVE AGENCY - MEANS, MOTIVE, and OPPORTUNITY - Book 9 & the Series Finale

THE TAKEN!/TANNER Series in order

THE CONTRACT: KILL JESSICA WHITE - Taken!/Tanner - Book 1

UNFINISHED BUSINESS – Taken!/Tanner – Book 2

THE ABDUCTION OF THOMAS LAWSON - Taken!/Tanner – Book 3

PREDATOR - Taken!/Tanner - Book 4

DETECTIVE PIERCE Series in order

MONSTERS - A Detective Pierce Novel - Book 1

DEMONS - A Detective Pierce Novel - Book 2

ANGELS - A Detective Pierce Novel - Book 3

THE OCEAN BEACH ISLAND Series in order

THE MANY AND THE ONE - Book 1

SINS & SECOND CHANES - Book 2

DRY ADULTERY, WET AMBITION - Book 3

OF TONGUE AND PEN - Book 4

ALL GOOD THINGS… - Book 5

LITTLE WHITE SINS - Book 6

THE LIGHT OF DARKNESS - Book 7

STERN ISLAND - Book 8 & the Series Finale

THE REVENGE Series in order

JOHNNY REVENGE - The Revenge Series - Book 1

THE APPOINTMENT KILLER - The Revenge Series - Book 2

AN I FOR AN I - The Revenge Series - Book 3

ALSO

THE EFFECT: Reality is changing!

THE FIX-IT MAN: A Tale of True Love and Revenge

DOUBLE OR NOTHING

PARKER & KNIGHT

REDEMPTION: Someone's taken her

DESOLATION LAKE

TIME TRAVEL TALES & OTHER SHORT STORIES

A VICTIM OF CIRCUMSTANCE
Copyright © REMINGTON KANE, 2018
YEAR ZERO PUBLISHING

This book is a work of fiction. Names, characters, places and incidents either are products of the author's imagination or are used fictitiously.

Any resemblance to actual events or locales or persons, living or dead, is entirely coincidental.

All rights reserved. Except as permitted under the U.S. Copyright Act of 1976, no part of this publication may be reproduced, distributed or transmitted in any form or by any means, or stored in a database or retrieval system, without the prior written permission of the publisher.

❀ Created with Vellum

Printed in Great Britain
by Amazon